JACK NOLAN

Dead Ends

Stay Strong!
Jack

First published by YCB Publishing 2019

Copyright © 2019 by Jack Nolan

All rights reserved. No part of this publication may be reproduced, stored or transmitted in any form or by any means, electronic, mechanical, photocopying, recording, scanning, or otherwise without written permission from the publisher. It is illegal to copy this book, post it to a website, or distribute it by any other means without permission.

This novel is entirely a work of fiction. The names, characters and incidents portrayed in it are the work of the author's imagination. Any resemblance to actual persons, living or dead, events or localities is entirely coincidental.

Jack Nolan asserts the moral right to be identified as the author of this work.

First edition

This book was professionally typeset on Reedsy. Find out more at reedsy.com

Authors Note

Dear Reader,

Thank you for picking up this book! It has been a rollercoaster bringing what you see to reality, but one I can say I would not regret stepping on. After having an idea and turning it into a reality and after bouncing back from unforeseen circumstances with my mental health. I can proudly say this is my 2nd novel and so far, has been a challenge to write but a piece of work I am glad to have accomplished. As every go getter knows, facing many defeats can only lead to one decision. That one decision is to take charge of the cards you have been dealt and to find your own way! No matter what your circumstances are, 'anything is possible'.

I'd like to give a special thank you to everyone who has been a part of the process of supporting me, on my mission to bringing this book to life! From the amazing cover design and photography created by Lisa Gee, Robert Cragg and the team at Studio G Photography. Along with the prop support, kindly provided by GM Airguns and their team! I can honestly say that these are the best in the business with the services they provide. What you see with my book cover would not be possible without their abilities to go above and beyond with their services and skills!

Also, to everyone that featured as a part of the production for the book cover and marketing materials, I would not have been able to pull it off without you guys! So I thank you very much, Graham Cheadle, Phil Jackson, Mark Bennett, Peter Nolan, Daniel Thomas, Brian Joyce, David Bowie (aka Boo) and Steven Gidwaney.

On a last note and before you dive into this novel, I would not have been able to produce the work you see today without the love and support of my family. Thank you Mum & Dad.

Stay strong and win!

Jack Nolan

Henry Slate Prologue

I'm sat here, in my bar, in my usual seat and I see these two youths come in. Aspiring young guns wearing them stupid, bright coloured tracksuits with no respect for a shirt and tie. My hands start to twitch as I overhear the scrote's mumbling about gangsters. I pick up my pint and take a swig. These youngsters amuse me, as they have no idea whose house they sit in, talking a load of tripe. "I know the gaffer to this place, Manchester Mafia Man, Henry Slate, he's ran this place for years. I know him through my Dad and we don't fuck about!" I scan his face, but still can't recall, feeling humbled I nod to my bar man. I walk towards the rowdiness of the cocky scum at my table and watch my league's eyes follow. "Fuck off old man!" the loud mouth shouts as the room falls still to the cocked sawn off behind the bar. I look to my friend and wink that everything is okay but I still feel the aggressive side to my retired nature. I look in the youth's eyes and see nothing but ignorance as he blindly stares into mine. Have I still got it? I question myself, "SMASH, I'm Henry fucking Slate," my pint glass shatters across his face, as he stands shaking in total disbelief.

Chapter 1

Past

Everyone assumes being a criminal is just like one of those gangster films, where there is a pecking order of those at the top, making all the decisions. Well it's not far from the truth, except the decisions I make change people's lives and this was one of those days where change was about to happen.

Monday morning, 1st September 1962. "Get them guns loaded, it's going to get hot!" Sat in the back of a white van, me and my boys were all hungry for action. Craig Connolly was one of the hot heads on the job, followed by his brother Jamie. Now the way I saw it, we were unstoppable. "Come on, get out the fucking van!" Ray had pulled up outside the Post Office. "Let's go Henry!" The three of us ran into the Post Office, guns blazing, letting off shots. It was our time to make some real money, separate from those above us. We were like the SAS, professionals, everything had to be timed perfectly and with an aim to be in and out in under five minutes.

I noticed this old lady with her grandson, both shaking in fear as

CHAPTER 1

the person on the desk froze. He reminded me of myself at that age, unaware of the real world. Tears streamed down his face and his hands were squeezing his ears tightly. BANG! BANG! BANG! A couple of shots left the chamber of my rifle as I tried to speed things up. I couldn't get that kid's face out of my head, I suppose it was just one of those occasions: wrong place, wrong time. "How long does it fucking take to get the money in the bag? Hurry the fuck up!" I screamed, losing my patience. "There's more in the back." "Leave it, let's go.... NOW!" As we fled, the old lady latched onto Jamie's rifle, creating a tug of war for the bag of cash. BANG! The old lady's body fell to the floor, thudding to the ground, blood dispersed just like our exit. The child's face looked straight into my eyes through my balaclava. I'll never forget that day.

Present

I love my daughter with all my heart and here she was on the phone, excitedly telling me about her latest role at the theatre. "Hey Dad, I got the part.... I was even up against some television actors, but somehow they chose me!" She told me that she was going out to celebrate with her friends and that we would catch up the following day. I'm a Dad you see and so proud of what she has achieved all on her own, without any influence from me. She's a beautiful young lady, just like her mother was, sharing the same blonde hair with none of that hair dying shit. A real natural beauty, her mum would have been so proud of her. Now the question you might ask, do I wish I'd have had a son, someone to take over the empire I have built? I do think about it at times but then I realize that I have many sons, an army of them in fact, and some of whom would probably do more for me than any blood line. I have been out of the game for some time now and hopefully no more blood will fall by my hand. I do still oversee the day to day shit, but I'm not the same ambitious young man I once was. Sometimes it still feels like the old days, seeing all the old faces and watching the new generation attempt to make their waves, but as long as there is peace on the streets for now, I must be doing something right.

I like to be invisible, to walk the streets without worrying who's going to end me. When you get to be a man of my age, in the life I chose, success means more than money. It's being right here in this moment and that's something these young ones don't seem to grasp. But I imagine I was probably like that myself at their age.

Now my brother, Chris, he took the path in the opposite direction to me. Fucking Pig!! As much as I can't understand why he chose that path, he has become useful to me. We have had our different beliefs, but when he joined the force he became mother's golden child, even though she never really respected a man in uniform. We did have some disagreements at times and he would always try to catch me out or slow me down in some way. Then I came up with the idea that if I fed him the crumbs to my world, he would rank up to detective faster than the system could handle and that was something I could also take advantage of. He wouldn't accept my money though, when all I wanted to do was look after my own, but he would accept my stories and the insights that I could feed him.

I noticed 'Sam the Knife' at my bar and approached him with a smug smile on my face. "Just like the old days hey Sam?" "Yeah, just like the old days, you won't be seeing that young one again. I could have let that gun go right off in his face." "I'm glad you didn't, it would have made a bit of a mess." Sam laughed and combed back the grey hair on his head. I knew he was thinking the same thoughts as me. "Well,

CHAPTER 1

you did make a bloody mess," Sam laughed and went on to say, "we're too old for this, we should get out of here and hit Miami like the old days." "Miami?" "Yeah Miami! Remember all those half naked girls on the beaches, drinking until we were past caring. The clubs, the drugs, the excitement Henry." "We've been and done that Sam, it's a new generation now and besides, I can't leave Rebecca, you know I put my family first." "Well, just think about it, you don't know how long we have left, we're getting old you know! Maybe I could make it a business trip." "Go at your leisure Sam, there's enough running around to do here, I'm supposed to be on my retirement." I grabbed the nearest cloth from the bar and wiped the blood off my hands. That's the last time I will have to clean up, I said to myself. Maybe Miami wasn't such a bad idea after all, I was due a holiday and maybe I could take Rebecca with me, it was her 23rd birthday coming up.

I felt my phone vibrate, it was a missed call from Rebecca. I looked down at my phone and noticed I had missed multiple calls from her, stupid phone! I must have knocked it on silent with all the commotion earlier. "What's wrong Henry?" "Nothing, it's just Rebecca, she's called a few times, she must want picking up!" It was only 1am, which was still fairly early for her to call. Maybe I should have sent someone to watch over her, but I just thought I was being too over protective. I am very protective since her mum, my wife, died giving birth and I promised to myself that I would not let anything ever happen to her. It still hurts when I think about it, maybe she was just too old to bore a child. It was my fault we had left it late, but I would never regret having her, she is the one pure thing I have in my life. A bark of a cough erupted from my throat as I spat thick red blood into the towel I was holding. Fucking hell! Sam was right about one thing, we didn't know how long we had left, but I knew my days were fewer than his.

I dialled Rebecca's number several times and it just rang out and kept switching to the stupid damn answerphone. Constantly having no answer started to unsettle me, as she would always pick up after a couple of rings. A voice message appeared, I held it to my ear. "Help! Help! No…. Please….don't…..please stop!! Ahhhh!! Ahhhh!! Help me, Dad….. Dad….." BANG! I dropped the phone to the floor, what had I just heard? Was my daughter being raped? Has she just been shot? My thoughts were all over the show, I was a mess!! "Arghhhh….No!!!" I roared like a lion, a fucking ferocious beast, how the fuck could this happen. Who? What? Where?? My brain was going into overtime. My baby, my baby!!!! I swept the empty glasses across the Bar with my arm, smashing them, as they slid along the tops to the floor. I fell to the ground onto my knees. "HENRY WHAT'S HAPPENED? CALM DOWN, CALM DOWN." "My baby girl is gone, my baby girl is gone and I don't know why. This can't be happening, it's not right, who would do this? Arrghh," tears fell. Sam pulled the phone to his ear and listened to the voice mail. "What the fuck!" Everyone in the room was looking at us, shocked at my reaction, but no one was yet to know what the fuck had just happened. My gang members felt unsettled and gathered around me. I felt the room shrink smaller and my heart stop. My breath stopped and in that moment, I was dead inside. Helpless and filled with emotion like I had never experienced. I felt hands around the side of my waist, picking me up from the floor. "Breathe!!…...Henry!!…...Breathe!!" I could hear Sam whispering down my ear as my eyes caught the light whilst trying to catch my first breath. Tears stained my face, no one had ever seen me in such a vulnerable position before. I heard Sam clearing everyone out of my bar. He held his arm around me as we sank against the bar, "listen to me, we will find whoever has done this…. look at me…..YOU ARE HENRY FUCKING SLATE and that now means death to whoever has done this and those involved." I couldn't respond, I literally could not speak, I felt my body

CHAPTER 1

shake and floods of tears fall from my eyes. "She's... my... baby." "I know, we will get this bastard." After I finally caught my breath, which felt even harder with my rotting body, I grabbed the phone, took a deep breath and called back. It answered to my surprise! "Listen to me you fucking evil mother fucking murderer, I'm going to find you and put my nightmare right there in front of you and make you beg for your fucking life. I'm going to end you. Do you even know who I am? I'm Henry fucking Slate, I own this town. There's no where you can hide, you murdering rodent."

I was clearly emotionally unstable, so the next day I called a meeting. All of my organisation were there, all of the Manchester gangs in my control. I scanned the army I had created and noticed one gang member missing. I was immediately suspicious. "You all know why you're here, you got the memo?" Sam the Knife spoke to the mob whilst I was sat on my throne. Still in shock about what had happened, my heart was skipping multiple beats per minute, as I kept looking at my phone and analysing my actions in disgrace. The one night I didn't send anyone to look out for her. I felt a burning sensation rise inside me as I unleashed another blood-filled cough into my handkerchief. I listened to Sam explain the situation, I also noticed people from my younger days were not in the room, I guess some lose respect the older they become. I rose to my feet like the man I once was and let all the power inside of me unleash. "Listen and listen carefully! I don't care how you do it, how you find this guy, but I want you to know from me….. HE RAPED AND KILLED MY DAUGHTER!! This is no business threat, this is clearly a personal execution to get back at me, so whoever gets their hands on him, I want him alive, so I can personally chop off his bollocks….. is that understood?"

I felt myself feel alive again after those words. I wanted this bastard so much, much more than anyone who I had conflicts with before. I picked up my phone and dialled Rebecca's mobile again, it answered but no one responded, so I gathered my thoughts. "Listen to me you evil fucker, where is my daughter? Where is she, you bastard?" Whoever was on the opposite side on my daughter's phone had heard my message clearly and ended the call. I just wanted her body, I couldn't just leave her where she was lay. I felt a pain in my chest again, the familiar stabbing pains that reminded me of how much of a failure of a father I had been. I should have been there for her when she was growing up. I gave her my best intentions, sending her to the best schools, the lot. I knew she would be watching from above in disappointment, right beside her mother. God this can't be right, how can someone do such an act to my girl unless mentally unbalanced. There are no principles in killing the innocent.

Sam approached me wearing a smart black suit. "Things will start happening soon Henry, everyone knows what's happened, the word is out." "I know", I spoke quietly nodding my head whilst pinching my lips with my fingers. "It's only a matter of time, have you spoke to Chris yet?" "No, not yet, only those that need to know, know." I knew where this was leading, but I just wasn't ready. "Well he will soon find out, he's got informers." I repeated myself, "I know."

I felt so weak, a weakness I had never experienced before. I felt my phone buzz in my hand, I looked down to a text message. 'Victoria Mill, Ancoats' the message read with one of those smile emojis at the end. "Sam, this bastard has sent me an address." Sam immediately scanned the phone with his eyes and I could tell he was anxious about the information we had just received. "We've got to go and search that place Sam." "I've not got a good vibe about this Henry." "Well get that old musket of yours, because we're going." "Right", Sam responded

CHAPTER 1

whilst he was sharpening his knife - the blade that made him his name. Sam was vicious back in the day, it's not like him to lose his bite, maybe he too was feeling the effects of time. Sam brought his nephew, Jason, into the circle and called him to get a car ready for us. Jason was a good lad, he didn't take after his uncle with his knife skills, but he could drive fast and shoot and that's all we needed, a driver and a damn good one.

Chapter 2

Past

1947

It was 22nd June 1947, my 11th birthday. I didn't expect much. Chris was 2 years younger than me. Our father worked on the streets and that's all we knew, we didn't ask questions or have any particular interests in what he did, because he would come and go as he pleased. Always on my birthday or any birthday, he would show his face with a gift, that's if my mother allowed it of course. They had left each other shortly after Chris was born, so we were mainly brought up by my mother and her family. They were hardworking, honest people, but still they lacked any real money to support us all. My mother had three sisters so we had a few cousins flying around, that we would normally get into trouble with. I didn't really like them to be fair, especially Eric, he was a bully and a couple of years older than us, a real nasty little shit.

My Dad entered the house where all my mother's family were, sat squashed together in the front room. Cards were on the walls and homemade decorations were plastered everywhere with my name on. "I can't believe how old you are, you're a little man," one of my aunties declared. "He's my little man, both my little men, aren't you boys," my

CHAPTER 2

father responded to the daggers in their eyes whilst winking at us both. "Henry, come here my boy." My father patted me on the head and ran his fingers through my hair, he revealed to me a box wrapped in brown paper. "Open it," he smiled. I tore the paper apart, curious to what was inside. Last year he got Chris a metal police badge, all shiny and pretty, that was pinned to the top he was wearing today. No one knew where it came from and there were suspicions amongst my family. I got down to the last piece of wrapping paper and a wooden box revealed itself. There was a lock on it that was easily opened. "Go on then, take it out, every cop needs a robber," he winked again at Chris. My eyes were overwhelmed at the sight of a big metal cap gun, a revolver replica that had cartridges for the caps to load into, it looked like a real gun and I was so excited. I placed my hand on the handle of the gun and turned my head behind me, my mother's face was mortified and so angry. The feel of this toy just felt right in my hands, the way the metal shined and the cylinder rotated after each time I pulled the trigger. "Don't shoot me, I'm your Dad, ha ha ha." He fell to his knees pretending to die. The other kids laughed, but I knew they were jealous, especially that knob head Eric. I pointed my toy gun towards his face and pulled the trigger, each time imagining his head blowing straight off!! Ahh!! Eric!! his name goes through me like an allergic reaction. Toffee nosed prick. "Right, put it away now Henry," my mother spoke abruptly but trying not to shout at me on my birthday, so I put it back inside the box and slid the lock. "I've got to go now champion, but happy birthday son and don't shoot your brother's eye out," he laughed gently and smiled wiping back his slick, black hair. Even though my Dad wasn't in our life much, he was a charismatic man, from the way he wore his black Crombie to his shirt and tie. I could see how my mother was in love with him at one time. As he left, my mother followed, "who wants tea?" she mumbled as she walked on behind him. I heard them arguing in the back about what he had just bought me, he didn't deserve it, it's just a boy thing, girls play with dolls and boys play with guns. I suppose she was upset with what it represented, I guess.

I peeked my eye through the door that closed behind them. "Who do you think you are, bringing things like that into my family home?" my mother squawked. "It's just a fucking toy, get over it, he's my son." There was a lot of frustration in the room. "My son! Well why don't you take him, feed him and care for him?" I heard a slapping sound that pierced my ears, but I couldn't see what had actually just happened. "I pay my fucking way don't I, I give what I can." "You think you're it, don't you? With your shirt and tie and fancy clothes, well piss off and get out of my house." My Dad walked out of the house and slammed the door behind him. I pushed open the door I was peering through and went into the kitchen where my mother was sat on the floor, in a pool of tears. "Go back in the other room," she shouted. "Go now!!" I noticed a purple mark on her cheek and in that moment, I knew exactly where that slapping sound had ended.

How could someone I had looked up to and admired be so cruel, was that really the right thing to do in that situation? I was only 11 and my view of the world was simple, if my Dad did it, it must have been for a good reason, even though in my heart I didn't agree. This woman was my mother, she had done so much for us, where my father had not. From that young age, I made a decision that I was my own man and even though I was only a boy, I didn't want to depend on anyone other than myself. I grew up quick and I chose not to see my father for a while. Chris didn't see, he was unaware of what the world was like, so I let him be. He was my baby brother and so long as he had me, he would be okay.

After a few weeks had passed and many days of playing cops and robbers, cowboys and Indians and whatever else we could think of, I decided to go into town by myself. I heard my mother was down to her last lot of savings and my Dad had stopped giving her money after my birthday. I felt responsible as the man of the house, I felt anger and passion inside me and knew I had to do something. I got to Market Street and noticed all the stalls, it was an amazing sight, people selling toys and underwear, fruit and veg. My mother wouldn't let me go into town, but that was in the past, I made my own decisions now. The city was booming and the streets were full of passers-by and salesmen. "Get your juicy pears, ripe bananas and sweet clementines," one of the stall holders shouted repetitively. I came across a stall that was selling bread, now I knew that would go well with a nice bowl of soup, so I looked at the stall and noticed the holder was distracted, talking to a customer. I ran towards the stall at full force, my little legs going like the clappers with my torn soles on my shoes hitting the ground. I held my arm out and snatched the loaf of bread from the table. I felt my heart beat quicker and quicker as I turned around heading for a home run. For the first time in my life I felt alive, a rush of endorphins filled my little mind and motivated me to do more. I quickly looked behind me to see the stall holder trying to catch up with me, but I was too fast. I got to my street and returned home feeling like a hero, I felt like Robin Hood.

Present

Jason arrived with the Range Rover outside the bar, Sam had arranged for a couple of boys to come with us, just in case we needed them. I felt slightly excited by the journey as I kept imagining pulling the trigger on this fucker and letting him taste the rage I was experiencing. I held my Smith and Wesson revolver close to my chest and rotated the cylinder, six shots loaded and waiting for their target. Sam carried his sawn off under his coat, it was just like the old days. "Drive faster Jason, step it up a gear," I shouted from the back seat. My eyes scanned the navigating system Jason had installed into the car, watching the miles count down, I felt my fingers twitch. "I'm ready for this", I told myself, there is no way this no mark can beat me, I've been in the game far too long. I looked at myself in the reflection of the car mirror and stared into my wrinkled face. How time had come and gone, I felt anxiety kick in. I felt like I could hear the ticking sound of a clock in my ears, every second passing becoming more valuable than the last. My breath became limited, so I squeezed the handle of my revolver and took a deep breath exhaling some stress.

"You're a bit quiet back there Henry" Jason knew what was going on, but he couldn't resist breaking the silence. "Leave it," Sam responded for me. I was quiet, but I was sinking into my thoughts, was she really dead, or was it my imagination? I did hear her screaming which sounded like she was fighting for her life and a gunshot go off. She didn't respond and then the call ended. Was she really dead? I kept asking myself, thinking of early conversations we had just had days before. I kept thinking of the past and it burnt me up inside. Memories which were so vivid they almost felt real, they were real, but you know what I mean. I felt transported back in time to that moment when she was a child, coming home to see her walk for the first time. I didn't know much about parenting or changing nappies, so I paid for a nanny to help raise her. After her mother died, I couldn't imagine myself with anyone else, it felt wrong and in a way almost guilty. My heart was so fixed, even though it had been broken into pieces. The doctors said it was rare case due to her falling ill in the process of having Rebecca, the build-up of the illness had caused her body to be too weak to give birth, but I'm sure there were other problems that I just didn't realise. I'm not really one

CHAPTER 2

to talk too much about my feelings or fond memories, as bad people are supposed to be heartless, aren't they?

My eyes noticed we were getting closer to our destination and I felt a build-up of blood and saliva at the back of my throat, irritating my tonsils, I spat into my tissue and wiped my lips. The sky was dark as we drove down the street towards an old mill. "You have reached your destination," the device said out loud, alerting us all. Jason stopped the car and we just waited for five minutes and stared into space. "Come on, let's go!" I coughed. "I'll get you closer," Jason suggested and revved his engine moving us towards the entrance. The car behind us followed and a few lads jumped out as we crunched the handles on the door. Everyone was packing and we were ready for any unexpected surprises.

I entered the mill, feeling explosive, my senses on high alert. I lifted my foot onto the step of the door entrance and barged the door open with my shoulder. "Still got it," I mumbled. "I think it was already loose." "Yeah possibly." "The hinges snapped off easily enough." Cheeky bastard, I knew I still had it and he knew it too. I held my revolver forward and cocked back the hammer, "Rebecca??" I shouted. "Henry, you know she can't respond." I pulled my gun towards Sam feeling distress. "Come on Henry we will find her." Feeling Sam's hand press against my back, pushing me forward gave me the shivers, it was gloomy inside the mill and my sight felt blurry. Continuing the slow walk forward, creeping up the stairs checking each floor with caution, we couldn't find anyone or anything. We eventually got to the top and amongst the dirt and grime on the walls there was graffiti that spelt the words *'this way!'* "What's all this?" "I don't know Sam, but come on let's keep going." I scouted the room. "No!!....No!!.... Please God, no!!!!" I fell to my knees in a state of despair. "Henry, what is it, talk to me?" I lay on the floor alongside my daughter, her clothes were torn with blood stains entrenched in her skin. I felt my eyes burn and my blood pressure rising. I brushed her hair gently, the numbers '1 9 6 2' were mutilated onto her stomach. I couldn't understand what sick bastard would do such an inhumane act like this, and to my beloved daughter. This was some fucked up shit, I grew with anger and all I could think about was pulling the trigger. I raised the gun to my head and fretted, "I've failed as a father." I cried uncontrollably, with the gun pointing to my head, then towards Sam, back and forth the revolver went. "Why is God punishing me? I know I've done wrong, but she was the only one thing I had done right." "Henry give me the gun." Sam placed out his hand and walked slowly towards me. His face was forlorn as a tear descended down his face, he wiped it with the sleeve of his jacket. "You see Henry, life's tough, it will bring you to your knees in the darkest of times, but this is not your fault." I felt my legs shake like I had never experienced before, I looked to the floor where my daughter lay. Why had God been so cruel, she was pure, innocent, beautiful and unaware of the dangers of the world. I was still listening to Sam talk as I pulled the gun away from my face. "What matters is what you do now Henry, what you do now, do you hear me Henry, it's okay to feel the pain, feel it, use it." Bang! I let a shot off into the air and felt my old wrists twitch. "Arghhh!! That's for the big man upstairs." I was the only person who could take life and life had been taken, but by another's hand.

Chapter 3

Present

I lost all sense of time, hours passed, days passed and I couldn't hear any thoughts in my mind but the year 1962 consistently repeat itself. My sleeping patterns had become disjointed, I was unaware of how much sleep I had had. I don't think I even slept at all for the first few days. I was sat in my bar drinking a bottle of vodka to myself and I heard the door squeak open. "Henry, you don't look great pal, you should have got some rest." It was Sam coming to pick me up, I wondered what time he would come. "I couldn't sleep." I felt almost motionless. "Do you remember when I first met you Henry?" I just looked at him and nodded in response. "It was right in here, you challenged me to a drinking competition and you won." I pulled a smile. I remembered that day well. "I promise you after today we will do the same again." "Thanks Sam, I'll let you know if I'm up to it." I looked to the empty bottle of vodka on the table and grabbed it… Smash!! "Bloody hell Henry." "Come on, you're right, it's time."

Seeing the hearse outside with my daughter's name written in flowers hit me, it felt like I was watching a film, where everything is staged, but the truth was, this was very real. I brushed my hand along the hearse and read her name that was decorated in white roses. I had brought her into this world and now she was lay inside this wooden coffin. No father wishes to see this sight in their lifetime, I should be gone first, not my beautiful Rebecca. I pulled out a tissue and wiped my eyes, I had not shed so many tears before, not since Jane.

I spoke to God this morning and said a prayer hoping that both my wife and Rebecca could hear. "I love you both my darlings" I whispered to myself as I followed Sam into the back of Jason's car. There were rows of cars following, mainly people paying their respects to my loss. We followed the hearse to All Saints Church, it was quiet and all I could see was the sight of black from people's suits to the early morning sky. After a 20 minute drive, we arrived at the Church. I looked around and there stood at least 30/40 people, mostly those who had been told about the latest series of events. Walking back towards the hearse, getting ready to lift the coffin, I could feel the weight on my shoulder and at that point I felt myself shake. I wasn't the tough person everyone believed I was. Beaten by the world literally, this was far worse than anything I had ever experienced. It goes through me to say the word 'coffin', but we lay Rebecca along a marble table.

I kept my words to myself and found the seat closest to her. The priest came in and did his routine of singing praises that I could not pull myself to mutter and then he went into a speech about life. Like he knew anything about life, when all he has done is spent his entire life reading books and singing songs. I had an instant disliking vibe towards him that caved in on me through my upset. "My children, we are here today to celebrate the life of Rebecca Slate." How he talks, like he knew her in a tone so soft. It grinded on me, but today wasn't about him or me, it was about my darling girl. I heard the sound of the organs start to play as everyone started to leave when the priest spoke his last words of irritating comfort. "My child, God works in mysterious and wonderful

CHAPTER 3

ways. He will be saddened by your daughter's exit but he will welcome her to the heavens with open arms and she will sit amongst him with the angels in the kingdom. You will see her again, that I can assure you." I didn't even respond, but who was he to talk to me about God and life? I can assure you, with what I have sinned I was definitely not going to make it to heaven. The only way I was to see her again, was in photographs and memories that lived in my mind.

They lowered Rebecca into the depths of the church garden, where there were other graves and amongst them was Jane. I made sure there was a place for her next to her mother. A space which I thought I was next to fill, there was enough space for my exit to be buried with them both though. When I was young I imagined my death to be like a Viking, to burn on a ship and drift out to sea, but to be with my family is where my heart will be, always. As the coffin lowered into the darkness of the ground I threw in a white rose, the only thing that was pure and innocent, just like my angel. "I'm so sorry Jane," I muttered. Sam gave me space, as I stood alone watching the dirt fall into the hole. "I hope she will bring you some company up there my girl." I felt the wind blow on my face and I felt the presence that they were both with me, this was their spirit comforting me. They say a real man shows his emotions, but I was yet to agree until all of a sudden, I felt tears fall from my face. "Why God??" I cursed again, I could tell he wouldn't be happy with me if he heard all the things I had said, but you know what, I hope he heard every single one of my thoughts for which I had angered.

People started to show their respects by throwing flowers into the grave and it meant a lot. Rose after rose, there soon became a bed of white that sat on top like wings of an angel, so white, so beautiful. As the dirt started to enter and the burying process began, I just waited, everyone had left all except Sam who stood a few paces behind me. I felt a drop of rain hit my face that broke my stare, it almost felt like a tear drop from heaven. Maybe it was Jane, who was to know. "You know she will always be with you Henry." Sam spoke with care in his tone. "I know," I responded, then a silence appeared again between us that became broken by the buzz of my phone.

I looked behind me, before looking at my phone and seen another figure of a man in black. It was Chris, he had not spoken a word to me all day and it pissed me off a little, but I guess he knows me better, that I like my own space especially at a time like this. I held my hand up to him and he nodded. 'Did you find what you were looking for?' I looked down to my phone and read aloud.

Past

A year had passed since my birthday and I was still active on the streets, pinching here and there. It was a Monday morning around 9am, I jumped out of bed before my mother headed off to work. She thought I was heading straight to school with Chris but I hadn't been going and especially not today. Chris was aware of what I was doing and even though he was a good egg, he did see the value, especially when I brought him back a chocolate bar. Stealing small things was easy, bread, butter and tins. All you had to do was make sure each shop keeper was distracted and that was it, simple. Running fast was the only skill set you needed if things got out of hand, but my luck had not run out just yet, thankfully.

I headed to the markets with a cocky smile on my face and at this time everything was busy. Business was booming you could say, everyone shouting at passers-by trying to flog their stock and then there was

CHAPTER 3

me, eyeing up the opportunity to make a snatch. I walked up and down Market Street a couple of times, waiting for the right moment. I wanted to make an easy steal because I felt tired from the rush to get here and there it was: the perfect chance. I saw this one seller in deep conversation, working his craft on a passer-by. He had socks dangling from his wooden platform table, he was doing well with a queue starting to form. 'Perfect' I thought to myself, this couldn't get any better especially with Christmas on the way. Those little bastard socks would keep me and our kid warm, a scarf as well I noticed, brilliant. I was about to take on my biggest lift, fuck it I thought, it's now or never and it was already a cold day.

I ran up to the stand and grabbed a bunch of socks and pulled at the scarf. 'Yes!,' ran through my mind, 'I've done it.' I began to run but there was people in my way, I pushed through until I felt a giant hand grab my arm. "Get off me, you bastard!" I screamed with the deepest tone I could, I didn't look back to who it was, I just kept fighting moving forward. I dropped the socks but still had the scarf wrapped tightly around my hand. "Hey, hey, calm down." I heard what I thought was a familiar voice, but my intentions were to get out of there. I fought with this arm that came around me. "Get off me, do you know who I am?" I kept shouting, repeating myself, becoming more and more furious. "Yes, I do, I'm your Dad!" I turned my head and froze in silence to the face of a slick, shaven face. I couldn't believe it! The crowd began to disperse. "Thief!" a man shouted. "Thief, you got that little brat." "My son is no thief." My Dad laughed with a huge grin on his face, whilst I was still in shock at the sight of seeing him. He dragged me and forced me to apologise to the man who wore a flat cap with crooked teeth.

I was confused, yet stubborn and feeling angry inside. I was so close to getting away with a good load. "Have you got anything to say to the man?" I looked away from him in disgrace. I couldn't believe it, my own dad making a fool out of me. Now the man had a clear sight of what I looked like, but he also became aware of where I had come from, whose offspring I was. I had no idea how I was getting out of this situation until my dad pulled out some change and paid for the gear that I had successfully stolen until he sabotaged my exit. What on earth was running through my dad's head? "Thanks Joe, it means a lot, your kid needs some discipline," the market trader responded. My Dad still had a tight grip on me and he picked up the socks and dragged me to one side. "Why aren't you in school?" he began to shout, loud enough so the man he had spoken to could hear. "I have to do something useful, don't I?" "By thieving hey? You're lucky I caught you, I don't think you're fit enough to get a good hiding off these lot out here," my Dad extended his voice once again and winked. I didn't understand why he winked, it just didn't make sense. He dragged me into one of the back streets shouting all sorts "I'll be giving you a belt myself, you don't steal out here!" my Dad repeated himself. "Do you hear me?" Once we were out of sight of the crowds and market traders, he began to laugh to himself, but then his tone and face changed. "Listen to me, you little fucker, why you doing that?" "Because there's not enough money, since you've been gone, it's been even harder." "Save me all of that shit, you sound just like your mother." I looked straight in my dad's eyes and held back the ball of saliva that I wanted to spit into his face. He was intimidating and, in his eyes, I saw for the first time the truth - he was an aggressive, old man, heartless I thought. "I'm not afraid of you." He grabbed me by the collar of my shirt and forced me up against the wall. "I know you're not, you're a Slate." My dad's face relaxed and he spoke softly. "Look son, the skill is not to get caught, do you really think I'm going to beat you for something I've been doing my entire life?" In that one sentence, he answered the questions to the thoughts I had had my entire life. I knew he was a crook, I fucking knew it. So why had he stopped me in my tracks? You'd think he would be proud wouldn't you, but still he had me pegged to the wall.

"Listen to me boy, you have a big future ahead of you. How are things at school?" "I wouldn't know, I'm hardly there." "Well do you like it?" He started asking me a list of questions that you'd think he would already know. "No, it's boring and useless." "Well can you count?" I nodded. "Can you read?" "A little, yeah." "Then that's that." He pulled a smug face. "Well if you want money you can come and work for me." Work, doing what I thought, he's a crook I thought. What possibly could he do for work, you don't just wake up in the morning and do work do you. If you're a thief, what more is there than socks and food. At this point in my life all I had known was the small things, the easy way, taking things here and there. "What do you want me to do?" I asked with excitement, as I had finally reconnected with my dad, on a level that I was yet to learn. He loosened his grip on me and I quickly wrapped the scarf around my neck and put the socks into my pockets. "Come on, follow me."

We walked back to the top of Market Street and passed all the stands. "Alright Joe!" The market traders all shouted and let on to my dad as he walked down the street. "Now why do you think you've not been caught in all of this time?" "Because I'm fast." "Yeah, there is that." He held his hand up to the traders and smiled. "Billy Jones, this is my son." "Oh aye, it is your boy." "He tells me he likes your bread." "Oh, he does." This man my father was talking too smiled and packed a loaf into a paper bag and passed it on to him. "Cheers, Billy." "You see son, all what your eyes can see, this is mine. Now I know you don't like learning, but this will be your new school now - the streets." "What do you mean, how can I work the streets." "You've been doing it already, I've watched you from time to time out here but now you're going to learn how to work." Learn how to work? All of this didn't make any sense, I'm sure he said I would be working for him. "Billy, my son's going to work for you tomorrow, he can earn back what he's took from you." "You're a funny man, Mr Slate, but yes he can help run my stall." "Good, that will be all, Billy." My father put his hand in the paper bag and tore some of the bread into his hands, taking a bite. "Go home now son, I'll be checking in on you now." He put his arm around me and shoved me in the direction of home.

Present

"Sam this bastard has just sent another text, the mother fucker, he's playing games." I shouted to Sam as my brother just watched and stood silently. Sam walked towards me squinting his eyes. "What's he said?" "Just look." "The cheeky little mother fucker, I've had it with this twat." I felt determined inside, although I could feel my blood pressure rising. I coughed into my tissue and wiped my mouth. "Maybe we should talk to Chris." "I don't want him involved in this - no police, just us." "He's still your brother at the end of the day, Henry, we could use his help." I didn't want him involved and, to be fair, his presence made me feel off, I imagined all of his minions running around his office with their plotting and making notes on the wall. This was a private affair between two gangsters. "This is family, Henry, your family. He could at least track the phone for us, possibly even find us a name." I stood for a few minutes thinking about Sam's suggestions. "Do this for Rebecca, Henry." I heard Sam's voice and I listened. He was right, I had to use all my resources to find this cunt. In this game of cat and mouse I was currently beaten and the odds needed to change. "For Rebecca!" I said firmly.

CHAPTER 3

We both walked towards Chris, feeling a sense of progress. "Chris!" I shouted clear. "I'm sorry about what's happened Henry," he responded. "I know," I nodded. "You know I'm always here for you brother." I watched his lips move and listened to his words of sympathy before revealing my true intentions of the conversation. "Look, Chris, I need a favour." "What is it Henry?" "This bastard who murdered Rebecca has her phone, he keeps texting me trying to fuck with my head and, to be honest, it's working." "I'll get my team to investigate." "No! No police, I'll handle this myself." I coughed again into the tissue in my hand and looked at Chris straight in the eye. "I need you to find out where this phone is, can you track it?" Chris was silent with his eyebrows slightly raised. "It would be against police procedures, but in this case, I will, but only this once." "Thanks brother, this means I'm one step closer to resolving the situation." We both looked at each other and I felt the love in his eyes hit mine. There's just something about blood that you cannot unbind.

Chapter 4

It had been a long week of unfolding events that were exasperating me. I was still trying to figure out the connection of the year 1962. I said a prayer to God, asking for the answers to reveal themselves but nothing, no signs were made, no eureka moments that burst with intuitive thoughts. I was blank and still felt the pain in my heart. My phone rang, it was Sam "hello!!! I have some news Henry." 'News?' I thought, 'what possibly could have happened that's new?' "Jason's had some news from some youngens, they've found one of the Chadds, the gang that didn't turn up at the meeting. We're going to bring him in?" "Alright, alright, bring him in through the back door and we will take him into the cellar." "Okay Henry, just like the old days." I put the phone down and smiled, finally the ball had started to roll and things seemed a little positive.

I heard a loud knock at the back door and jumped from my seat with a glass of brandy in my hand, I took a large swig which burned my throat, I could feel it mixing with the blood that kept coming up. I coughed a few times and spat into a corner, I had run out of tissues and there was no time for getting one, the cleaner will sort it. First things first, this Chadd was my priority, I opened the lock on the door and there stood Jason and Sam with a few other lads, with this man tied up. He must have been as old as Rebecca was or maybe a couple of years older,

CHAPTER 4

say early 30s. He had short back and sides and big, blue eyes, he looked like a handsome lad, but that was about to change, literally. I smashed my glass in his face and kneed him in the groin. "You little fucking rat!" I snarled, growing with aggression. "The rest of you boys can go, Sam, Jason you're with me." The youngen wriggled with his legs tied and fell onto the floor. Before the boys left they joined in with giving him a good old-fashioned kicking. The youngen was gasping for his life, crying and begging. "Right, get him up, get him up now!! Let's see if this little bitch has anything of value to say." Jason pulled him up and sat him on a bar stool. "Don't you fucking move." I looked at the boy's face that was covered in blood from my glass, slits in his face started to gush with blood.

Sam pulled out his set of knives and lay them on a barrel in the cellar. The black mould on the walls resembled the youngen's body, beaten black and blue. I felt the blood rush around my body as I felt reminded of my past. All the habits I had acquired over a life time were hard to shake off and even though I could sympathise with the youngen, I didn't hold back at all, not even for one second. "I don't know what you want," the youngen cried. "Why didn't your crew come to the meeting hey?" Sam punched into his stomach. "I didn't know there was a meeting." Sam pulled a knife from his set and waved it in his face. "Don't fucking lie to me, I don't have time for your lies." Sam viciously stabbed the knife into the youngen's leg. "Arghh" the boy bellowed. "Ain't so tough now, are you?" The young one whimpered like a child. "What's your fucking name?" I spoke firmly. I didn't know who this lad was, not that his name was of any importance, but it's common courtesy to know who you're talking to. "Spike," he muttered with tears streaming down his face. He carried a childlike nature about himself. "Listen to me Spike, I'll put a spike through you if you don't tell me who murdered my daughter. I know your lot was involved, so who is he, where is he and why did he do what he did." His leg started to shake with blood and piss leaking down his trousers. "Speak, you little shit." Sam pulled out another knife much bigger than the first one. "I'll gut you, you fucking rodent, that's all your type are and you've fucked with the wrong elders." "Listen to me Spike you're so far down the fucking food chain, you don't realise who sits at the top, you're nothing but a shrimp eating the plankton of our backs." Spike started shaking, he was clearly terrified of the situation he was in. "I don't know, I don't know, you're right, I'm just a shrimp. I don't know anything, I'm not valuable enough to know what's going on, nobody tells me anything." "Agreeing with us isn't going to save your fucking worthless life, answers now!" The boy started to irritate me, avoiding sharing what he knew. "Do you even know who I am?" "I think it's Henry?" He squinted his eyes. "Yes, that's right and it's Henry fucking Slate to you." I slapped him across his blood-filled face and wiped my hand on his top. "Who is your leader, whose idea was this?" "I can't, I fucking can't… they will kill me." I nodded to Jason and Sam. "Well we will fucking kill you, we don't fuck about." Jason punched the fuck out of him until he was moments away from his last breath as Sam then went on to torture him with his handy skill set. He hit all the right limbs with his blade causing immense pain. "Enough!!" I shouted over the noise of intense screams.

I pulled out my revolver from the back of my pants and loaded one shell into the cylinder. "Are you fucking watching?" I shouted. "You're a tough bastard so I'm going to give you a chance, one in fucking six." I pointed the gun to his head and pulled the trigger "Crunch!!" The gun rotated, loading the next shot. "Well, looks like you're in luck," I laughed. "There's only five shots left and one of them is for you." "You're fucking mad," Spike spat blood from his mouth that reminded me of what was brewing inside of me. "Fucking tell me now!!" "I don't know, I've told you all I know." "Agreeing with me and saying you don't know shit, isn't

CHAPTER 4

resolving the situation you're in." I pushed my revolver into his mouth and screamed down his ear, I could feel myself turning back into the old me. Crunch! Crunch!! I pulled the trigger again, rotating the cylinder twice. His throat started to gag on my barrel and he started moving his head left to right shaking it up and down. "Okay! Okay!" he mumbled, I couldn't make out what he was saying so pulled my revolver from his mouth and listened carefully. "Listen to me old man, FUCK YOU!" Spike laughed like a lunatic with tears streaming down his face. BANG! I pulled the trigger and blew his fucking head straight off!! The balls on this mother fucker, for someone so young, his naivety had just ended his life.

It had been a long time since I had killed a man and inside I did feel a little bad but I had no empathy towards this kid as he had clearly been involved with the death of my daughter. I could feel the warm spray of blood that splattered onto my face, I wiped it off with my free hand and looked to Sam. "He's not going to talk now is he, what are we going to do now?" "Something will come, I feel it." I pulled out my phone and took a picture and sent it to my daughter's phone, your next I typed, feeling a sense of premeditated accomplishment. One less horrible fucker in the world you could say, or one down and one to go. I didn't care about how many people I had to go through to get to this guy, I'd destroy their whole gang if I had too and I had the man power to do so. "Boys, clean this mess up." I passed the gun to Jason.

Past

It was Tuesday morning and again I followed my routine of waking up before eight to hit the stalls. It felt strange, as I walked towards Market

Street, as this would be the first time I would be doing some honest work. I'd still be keeping my eye out though, for any opportunities that may come my way. I was excited as I knew I could do better than Billy Jones, even though he was a grown man, he was slow and talked people to death which is what made stealing from him so easy in the first place. He became distracted and caught up in his own sales pitch that left opportunities open for people like me. Billy also took a liking to people too easily and gave them more than he received, with the hope people would spread the word about his breads, pastries and cakes.

When I arrived at the stall Billy had just finished setting up his stand. "Alright" I burped, swallowing a gulp of saliva. He ignored me, the ignorant, fat prick, so I spoke up again. "Have you seen my dad?" "Yes, sorry I was just in my own world then." "Where is he?" "I'm not sure, but you do remember your working with me today, thief." Billy sniggered. The cheeky bastard, even though I was young, I still knew a dickhead when I saw one. It would be a long day ahead I thought, spending my time with this guy. What was I to learn from him, he was just a market trader, nothing special. As time began to pass, people started to look and examine Billy's stock, I couldn't understand why; this stuff was high quality and fresh from this morning's ovens. I knew this because I had eaten so much of it and it tasted even better when it was picked by your own hand. I see a beautiful girl come up to the stall, her hair was naturally blonde, she was young just like me. I could never forget those eyes, they were bright blue and I couldn't stop staring at her as she approached me. "Can I have a loaf please?" she smiled at the end of her sentence and I felt lost for words. Billy was distracted so I just gave it to her. "It's okay, here just take it." "Thank you," she paused "but I cannot just take things without paying for them." She was so mature for her age, even though I didn't know her I could tell she was intelligent and more importantly she had morals, she was definitely high class. I

CHAPTER 4

smiled as she placed some coins in my hand and asked of her name. "It's Jane" she laughed "I must go now" and away she went. I couldn't believe her beauty and I certainly wouldn't forget her face.

It was around 10:30am and the streets were becoming busier. Business was booming and I began to shout and hail at customers "come on over, these are the freshest pastries and breads you will ever taste that won't be too hard on your pocket." You would not believe the amount of shit that came out of my mouth and I didn't care, I took a liking to this selling thing. I got a buzz every time I sold something and I had no idea what I was doing, I pocketed some change into my left and some for Billy in my right. He had a set price structure but who cares when you're moving stock fast. "Slow down kid, you're moving too fast!" "It's what I'm here to do isn't it?" "Yeah but you'll make mistakes." "Shut up old man and let me do what I know." I didn't care what he said, I was making more business and creating more attention than he was. Getting people in and getting them out, it was like one big pantomime, a big act I was putting on, talking shit and selling it too. After a couple of hours had passed I was exhausted, my throat was dry and I was tired. It was a full on first day, but I couldn't wait to get my first pay.

"Billy, we're going to have to close, we've sold out." "Kid I can't believe this is your first day, you've got some talent, I'll give you that." I felt humbled by his compliments as this was the first time I felt I had received any kind words. I see my dad walk by in the corner of my eye and I felt a sense of achievement. I couldn't wait to tell him the news, but he had already realised from the emptiness of the stand. "Looks like a successful day our kid." "Yeah, he sure has some moves" Billy responded. I couldn't hold in my desire any longer so I just let it out "where's my fucking money then, Billy Bob?" I cupped the day's earnings I had made and poured it into Billy's hand, my father and Billy laughed at my response. Billy scanned the coins and put them in his pocket and pulled out a pound. "Are you fucking serious?" "Watch your mouth boy!" my father shouted. "Is this a joke, I've worked my arse off for you all day and you give me peanuts." "You've had your earnings boy, the missing bread, the lost takings I've had through you." I was angry, in fact I was more than angry, I was furious I had been making this fat prick money all day and he had the cheek to throw one coin in my face with a smile on his. My dad just stood and watched my reaction, I could never get why he didn't say anything in that moment. He was just quiet and shook Billy's hand "thanks for watching over my boy" he said and grabbed me by the shoulder "come on, I'll walk you home."

I wanted to punch that fat bastard's face in, who the fuck did he think he was? After about five minutes of walking back on my route home, my dad broke the silence. "What did you think of your first day at work?" "I'm really not in the mood to talk." "Hey, I'm not your mother, when I ask you something you fucking answer," my dad snapped with aggression and I soon realised how alike we were. "It was good until that fat prick didn't pay me fair." "£1 is a lot of money for a boy of your age" my father's eyebrow raised. "£1.00? I made him more than a £1.00!! He must have made at least 50 plus, more even today, come on dad, the cheek." "Well what have you learned then?" "Never trust a fat prick and that people don't value me." I pulled out a bunch of change that I had hid from Billy and shoved it in my father's face "and that he should have never trusted me." My father's eyes lit up and he took the change off me. "That's my son, but tell me one good reason why I shouldn't give this back to him tomorrow." "Because its mine Dad, I made it."

"I know you did, but who got you the job?" "You?" I shrugged. "Then this money is ours, I did say you can work for me." "Okay Dad, for you I will, but for no one else, ever again. Why feed someone else when you can feed your own." "I'm proud of you son." I felt a sense of pride even

CHAPTER 4

though I had been pissed off that Billy had the cheek to pay me one fucking pound. Even though I had stolen from him, it was the principle, the fucking principle. "Tomorrow I'll get you a stand and you'll sell whatever I get you" "alright Dad, see you tomorrow." My dad handed me some change as we came to the beginning of my street. "See you tomorrow, Dad." I saw a smile on my father's face and it made me feel like a man, I was proud.... I was a Slate.

Chapter 5

Present

When I arrived home, I ran a bath for myself and threw my bloodstained clothes onto the floor. I soaked my head under the water before scrubbing my bloodstained skin, then sank back into the warmth of the hot water. I left my mobile on the side of the bath tub just out of reach of the water. After a couple of peaceful, undisturbed minutes, my phone started ringing. "Hello, Henry we've found the location of the phone, it's at 24 Holkham Close in Ancoats." It was Chris and he was straight to the point. It was 10pm at night and he had been late on his delivery of the information, as 10pm was out of office hours for sure. I was frustrated with the time but he insisted that his contacts had just found the location. "I'll come around and pick you up, we can go down together?" "No thanks Chris, you've done quite enough and that's just what I need, thanks Chris."

I jumped out of the bath tub and kicked my clothes to the side, grabbing a towel as I went. I could feel the cold air hit my skin as I rushed into my bedroom to get some clothes on. I dialled Sam's number hoping he would answer, "alright Sam it's Henry, we've got the location of

CHAPTER 5

Rebecca's phone." "Brilliant, it's about time, I'm just in the middle of cleaning up this mess." "Ah right, just leave whatever you're doing and we will sort it tomorrow. Get Jason to pick us up and get some lads ready, we might just need them." "Okay, I'll send him over now." Things were finally picking up and we were moving one step closer to this bastard. It was the most frustrating game of chess I had played in a long time and I was about to move my knights in for an attack, metaphorically speaking of course. The game was on and all I imagined myself doing was emptying all my rounds into this cunt.

I threw a fresh suit on and grabbed a box of bullets for my revolver and shoved them into my pocket. I felt my phone vibrate in my free pocket, it was a text message from you know who. 'You think you can scare me, you old wrinkled prick!' I sneered as I read the words out loud to myself. 'Just you wait, I'm coming for you, you fucking horrible no good bastard.' I sent the text message in anger, without realising how foolish I had just been. I was hoping he didn't acknowledge the mistake I had just made. I heard a beep outside from Jason's car, so I walked out pumped up and ready for the world. The date 1962 flashed once again in my mind, focus Henry, I told myself. "There is no time for distraction's now" I whispered to myself as I walked towards the back of the car. "Pistol," I croaked to Jason as I felt a build-up of bloody phlegm in my chest. Jason handed me my revolver that he had polished, it almost felt like new in my hands, I started to load it with shells before thanking him. "So, it's 24 Holkham Close, isn't it?" Sam muttered to me. "That's just outside Manchester, I know where it is." Jason professed in a deep voice.

The car moved fast and I noticed the cavalry behind us, the backup we needed if things got out of hand. I was reminded of how far and how powerful I had become, from the dirty streets of Manchester to running the most sophisticated organised gang in the city. Having that control over my men was an adrenaline rush, like no other drug you could imagine. We drove down Oldham Road but got stuck in a traffic accident. I felt anxious about the time it was taking, as the more time we spent on the road the less time we had to catch this bastard. I could feel my heart pounding; my blood pressure was surely rising. My patience began to wear thin with every second that passed by. "Come on Jason, move this fucking thing." "Relax Henry, we've got the element of surprise." "Just drive." "The last thing we want is any attention." "I know, I know" I gritted my teeth until I felt the motion of the car move, Jason accelerated the car forward. "Fuck me, it's about time." "Right, when we get in there, I'm just going to straight up shoot that fucker in the face." "We don't know Henry, we just don't know what to expect, remember to keep your emotions in check will you." Sam was right, I had begun to pick up the amateur habits of letting my emotions fuel my actions. I had to relax and stay cool, but I could feel myself fidgeting. I closed my eyes and rested them until the car came to a stop. In my mind, I could see my beautiful wife and Rebecca, a reminder of why I was here.

We arrived at a small estate where only a couple of houses followed on from each other in a square shape. 'Holkham Close', a sign read on one of the houses at the front. Jason rolled our car into the avenue with our back up right behind. I placed my revolver in my jackets holster and stepped outside of the car, counting each house number. "There it is boys, 24 Holkham Close." We walked hastily towards the house, just the three of us, whilst our back up waited for a signal. The street was deserted and only our presence was known, it was quiet and seemed like the perfect place for a hide out. Jason was a big lad and he put it to some good use, as he kicked down the front door of 24 Holkham close, it was like watching a bread stick snap as the door flew off its

CHAPTER 5

hinges. I went straight for my revolver and aimed it upwards, the metal touching my nose, whilst Sam held his Colt 1911. We were old school, Jason was new school, holding a Glock. Me and the boys heard the sound of some type of porno playing somewhere in the house. As we searched high and low for the bastard, it was soon evident no one was here. I walked into the front room of the house and could not believe my eyes. The sick twisted bastard had recorded my Rebecca, it was her screams we could hear playing as we searched the house. "Arrghhhh" I grabbed hold of the television and smashed it onto the floor. The sick bastard, he had been pushing my buttons, but by far this was something I had never expected. Seeing the images of my beautiful girl tied up and being abused was just horrific, I smashed the room up until there was nothing left. Whilst trying to gather some thoughts from what I was dealing with and amongst the mess, I came across Rebecca's phone lay on top of two photographs, one an old lady and the other a Post Office.

At first, I didn't have any idea of what was going on. This was like some kind of psychological and emotional rollercoaster I was on and Sam and Jason were coming along for the ride. "I can't believe he's not here! Look, what the fuck is this?" I put my gun back into its holster and handed the photos over to Sam. "What does all of this mean?" I felt a tear of frustration and anger roll down my face. Sam turned the photos over and noticed some writing on the back, "now can you see?" it read. Could I see? I couldn't see shit, other than this mother fucker taking the piss. "Can't you think of anything Henry, these seem like clues." I took the photos off Sam and gave them another look, but my mind was clouded with what I had just witnessed and I was spiralling out of control with the circumstance I was in. "Come on Henry, we best get out of here." "Someone should stay and watch the house in case he comes back." "Okay Henry, I'll get someone on it." "Maybe we could ask around and see if any of his neighbours know who he is."

"Yeah" I replied, "we will wait in the car." Me and Sam walked back to the Range Rover and sat on the back seats. Before Sam got inside he nodded to the other car that everything was okay and that they could leave. I sat there feeling so frustrated and tormented, I ran my hands through what was left of my hair and sighed "why me? I'm tired of this cat and mouse bull shit." "I know," Sam put his hand on my knee and spoke out "you've got to think Henry, come on, talk to me. There's got to be something in these clues that can help jog your memory." I looked at the pictures and focused on the old woman's face, I recognized her vaguely, or so I thought, but what was with the Post Office? What was my connection to this old lady? How was I supposed to know her? What was the purpose and meaning of all of this?

"What are you thinking Henry?" "I'm blank, all I've got is 1962 embedded in my head and I was just a young man at that age, a fucking kid."

"I know, but what about this Post Office?" I looked at the Post Office and it just looked like any other Post Office. I started to think back to my youth and then I had a moment of realisation. "I did do a job on a Post Office, it must have been my first job, yeah I'm sure of it." I looked back to the photo of the old lady "She was there at the Post Office, fuck me, it can't be. This woman got shot by Jamie Connolly, but I don't understand, why is this guy so bothered about an old woman." "Fucking hell Henry, your first job and someone gets killed. That is fucking amateur." "It wasn't me though, it was that Jamie, she grabbed onto his rifle." "You best keep thinking Henry." I decided to call up the Connolly brothers to see if they had any trouble, it was my intuition ringing inside of me but I got no answer. I looked through my daughter's phone to see if there were any sicker fucking clues this guy could have left, there was a picture of two figures hanging. I zoomed in and made out who they were, you guessed it, it was the Connolly brothers who I hadn't seen in

CHAPTER 5

years. There were four of us on that job, Ray - the driver..... oh fuck, the last time I saw him he was writing a book about all the adventures we'd been on. I fucking knew it was a bad idea, even though he assured me all the names had been changed. The fucking driver, where was he then if the Connollys were gone? Then it's me, is it, next in line? It seemed this guy knew everything about me, but what did I know about him? Some fucking small time, wannabe gang leader of the Chadds.

"Fuck me Henry, we best find out what the connection between this guy and this old woman is, it's probably a family connection. That's the only thing I can think of." "Yeah, that's true, we need to find out a fucking name though Sam, so we know who the fuck I'm going to be killing! It's pissing me off how fucking invisible this guy is, like he knows all our moves." "Is there anything else you can remember mate? Every detail counts now." "There was a boy, ever so young, I'll never forget his eyes, they were big and brown." "You should have killed the kid." "I was a kid myself back then, a stupid fucking kid. It was me who suggested the Post Office when the Connolly brothers were planning a job. It was supposed to be easy, a smash and grab, just whatever was in the tills, a straight in and out. That's when I learned not to do work with people you're not 100% on." "As bad as it seems, it probably makes sense why he has done what he's done, he probably thinks an eye for an eye." "But why now, all these years later?" "That's something that nobody knows." I fell silent in deep thought, what was I to do? I knew I had enemies, but all had been seen too, either paid off or dead. It had been a long time since I had any conflicts and this one I had grown mentally tired quite quickly. To be honest with you, I was vulnerable and exposed and for the first time someone had been running rings around me, hiding in the shadows of my sight, for all I know he could be watching us right now. I felt Rebecca's phone vibrate in my hand, yet again another text message. 'Did you find what you were looking for??' Fuck sake, I felt like I was on the urge of a mental break down with this fucking kid. "Have you seen this?" I addressed Sam. "Fuck him Henry, he's just trying to get in your head, you should try the same." "Yeah, you're right" I grimaced. 'Listen to me, you rat, I'm going to fuck you up like I did to your little friend! Face me, you coward, I will find you...FACT!!'

Past

The day had finally come, I was so excited, I was working with my father for real. I had no idea what to expect or what to do. I walked via Tib Street to meet him on Market Street and there he stood in his black Crombie. He looked cool and clean shaven with his slicked back hair, I was proud to call him my Dad. The fact he let me be my own person was something no other kid of my age could be. I was excited to learn how to become a man. I walked up to him and looked him straight in the eye, "Dad, let's make some fucking money!" To which he reacted with a cold slap across my face. "Don't you ever swear at me boy or I'll send you straight home to your mam." Fuck me, I thought to myself, my cheek was red raw, from that I learnt my first lesson on the streets. Respect was everything and to keep your words few, well clean, especially when talking to a grown man even if he wasn't my father. Beside his leg was a suitcase, which he held with a firm grip. "Now you listen here boy and listen good, you see this case, you don't let anyone come near it or take it, do you understand boy?" I nodded and smiled with curiosity as to what was in the case. We walked down Market Street and I stood tall, looking at all the market traders like the men they were. Stalls owned by us, I knew I was to own these streets one day and that's exactly how I looked at each and every one, with

CHAPTER 5

patience to one day have.

A girl caught my eye as we were walking, she was pretty and blonde. It was the same girl who had bought bread from me a few weeks back. How could I forget that face, a thing of pure beauty, I felt my stomach turn inside at the sight of her. For the first time, I did not feel in control and a frog sat at the back of my throat. "Hello Jane" I croaked with a smile. As she walked by me, she noticed my eyes lock with hers. "It's Henry, isn't it?" "Yes" I replied feeling slightly mystified on how she picked up my name as I did not pass it on, she must have heard one of the workers call for me, or maybe my name was becoming present amongst the streets already. My ego raised with the question behind how she knew my name as silly as it was. "What are you doing today?" I asked with a hidden agenda, wanting to take her out or even walk her home. I wasn't the smoothest of talkers but I knew what I wanted. Businesses, money and this beautiful girl one day, but time could only tell and I was new to this type of game but I was going to win. "I have errands to run for my mother, she's not been too well." "I'm sorry to hear, perhaps I could walk you home later after you finish your running around." "Perhaps" she smiled. "I'll meet you by your stall later," "Sounds good" I responded with a smile on my face awaiting the clock to tick away quickly. I walked with a spring in my step to catch up with my dad, dragging his suitcase forward.

"What was all that about?" my dad had a stern look on his face that followed with a snigger. "Women are distractions at your age, fuck them and see them off, she will drain you like a witch." I was only a child and I remember this moment in my life so vividly, I just ignored him as I didn't know what to say, I just kept my head down and kept trailing behind him. I started to think of my mother, she sprang to mind as Dad made that comment, is that why they weren't together anymore?

Is she really a witch? I questioned myself. Fuck it! I hadn't time for that type of thinking, work had already begun and soon my business mind started to race. "What's in that case then Dad, what's all the fuss about it?" "Don't ask questions that are not for you to ask." "Well where are we going then?" "You'll see my boy, it's a personal errand of my own." My dad winked at me like he was looking forward to the events of the day. I had no idea where we were going, we had passed Market Street and made a few shortcuts down back streets I had not been down. We then came to a pub that was quite secluded, The Tavern it was called. We walked in and there was sat a bunch of my father's friends, well associates you could say. "Where's Jimmy" shouted my dad. "He's in the back" one of the men responded, "nice one mate," my dad dragged the case along the sticky, wooden floor into the back room of the pub where a big man stood leaning over a pool table about to finish on his last shot. "Jimmy, here's the load" my dad grinned and both of them started laughing, like there was some joke I missed. "Is this your boy then?" "Yeah it is, he's a little bastard but a grafter." "He's definitely got your blood in him then." "For sure he has." My dad picked up the suit case and placed it on the pool table. "Watch the fucking green, you'll pay for it." "It's fine, wind your neck in." Jimmy put his fists up to my dad and pretended to punch at him. "You know how I rumble Robert, these hands, these hands are weapons." I laughed, breaking my own silence as the two started to discuss business. "Shut it you, or you'll get it as well." Jimmy smiled softly. "Shouldn't your lad be at school?" "This is my schooling" I replied. "The boy speaks!" Jimmy laughed and put down his cue on the table. "Well boy what do you think I am?" "An educated man" a grin revealed from Jimmy's face "and what do you think I do?" "Business??" "and what type?" "The type that is none of mine!" My father and Jimmy laughed. "You've got a good one there."

"He's a good lad." "Have him work a day with me." "He's too young

CHAPTER 5

Jimmy, he's still learning the streets." My dad looked up from counting the money that sat on the table. "We can't be having him be a waste of talent, from next week he will work the bar." "But Jimmy he's my lad, he needs straightening up first." "Boy, leave me and your father be, we have some business to discuss." I felt a slight shake of nerves as I didn't know how to respond to the conversation that involved me. I was excited though, I could tell Jimmy was an important man and I wanted to be where the money was, and in that room was a fuck load of it. Money that I need to get to the root of!

Chapter 6

Present

Jason jumped back in the car and shared his news, "Right, a lot of them were scared to talk to me, but one old guy mentioned that there is a group of lads who go in and out of the place and it belongs to someone called Kyle." Names are something that make it far easier, my eyebrow raised "you got a surname Jason?" "Harrison!" "Well next time give me the full fucking name you idiot, Kyle really narrows it down, doesn't it?? Fuck me!!" "Relax Henry, we've got something now, something rock solid." Sam smiled with a sparkle in his eye, whilst pocketing his 1911. "Let's get back to our place to make the calls that we're having a meeting."

The drive home was quiet, but it did not mean I was at peace even though we had just got this evil fucker's name, as my daughter and two associates of mine were still dead. I always cut off loose ends, which is why I've lasted so long on the streets but God must be cursing me with all these circumstances or maybe it's the devil himself, either way I could not stand this game of bullshit any longer. I was still grieving for my Rebecca and some days dragged with pain and others couldn't come quick enough. Tears ran down my face as my image of control

CHAPTER 6

had been broken, I rested my head forward and wiped my eyes with my fingertips. Each tear I cried, was for every regret I had.

Sam turned his head and spoke softly "you're going to get through this Henry, inch by inch." I wiped my face and stared back into Sam's eyes with rage "I'm going to kill him, I'm going to wipe them all out, whether it be all at the same time or one by one…. I will kill them all!" "That's the Henry I know, soak it up pal, we are nearly back on home soil." Sam offered a cigarette and I gladly took it. I didn't care anymore and that's when they say a man is most dangerous and I would certainly be proving them right. I inhaled the cigarette deeply, holding it in before releasing it. I could feel it burning my throat, mixing with my broken body. I knew time was limited for me and the clock was ticking, my days on earth were numbered, I prayed to God and the devil that I would make a deal with any of them to just give me more time to complete my last mission, one last purpose to do what's right in my eyes.

The sit down had been arranged and the leaders of all the other gangs in the city were present in the room "Now some of you may have heard that I had retired, some of you may have even thought I was dead, but rumours of my demise were as they say, grossly exaggerated. You all know why you're here and I assure you I will honour my word, but every fucking one of you hear this…. I want the Chadds' fucking heads on a stick and I want to know where they are and any information that you can give me. We are all businessmen and you've all prospered under my leadership, but know this, there will be no money and no drugs until I find the Chadds. Business is business we all agree but killing my daughter is more than a business acquisition, it's a personal execution aimed at me. I've never questioned your loyalty, I only expect that you treat this as a loss of your own as if it was your daughter who had been killed and trust me I would not wish this on anyone. Now I want this done right, burn these fuckers to the ground." I watched as they shook their heads in disbelief whilst sipping on their pints. One of the men spoke up, "a war is bad for business." "Who the fuck do you think you are talking to, you cunt? This is Henrys Slate's daughter we're talking about!" Sam pulled his 1911 and pointed straight at the man's head. "Easy now Sam, he's right, war is bad for business, which is why I am allowing you all to take over their stash houses. This is something you can discuss among yourselves, all I care about is my fucking revenge!" Sam released the tension in his grips and put the pistol deep into his trousers. "That settles that then, do I make myself clear?" I spoke firmly, maintaining the position I had spent a lifetime to acquire.

The heads of my organisation started to leave after I finished speaking, I looked upon them and the kingdom I had built and still I felt emptiness inside. No sons by blood and no family to leave all of this to, no real blood. There was Chris, but he was a high-ranking detective far away from this life. I guess I'm the last of my generation, a dinosaur awaiting extinction, but this old man still had a fight in him, well that's what I told myself to get through the pain of loss and closely ending mortality. "Let's raid one of Kyle's stash houses, fuck it!" I shouted to Sam. "We already have the lads on it Henry, maybe we should take a step back to rethink our plans and wait for news to come." "I can't fucking wait Sam; my time is limited on this cunt. The only way to find a monster is to look under the bed and I'm the biggest monster in the city." "He could be anywhere, we need to prepare for our next move." "This is our next move Sam!!"

I let some time pass to think about what Sam had said and walked towards my seat in the bar, you could taste the smell of cigarettes on your tongue. Sam stared at me, puffing away in disbelief at the fact that not only was I running out of time before the police could catch up

CHAPTER 6

to us, but I was dying and the smell of cancer brushed my face as Sam exhaled every puff, in a desperate need to distinguish the stress of the situation. It was real and another reality I had to face, my throat caught dry and I belched a blood ridden cough. "Fuck sake Sam, I can't take this shit. The TV of Rebecca, it's scarred me for sure, we need to get our hands on the footage that the police have of that night and get a clear picture of who this guy could be." "You're right there Henry, but once we've got the face of this cunt, it will still be a tough one." "But at least we will know who we're hunting." I placed my blood ridden tissue on the empty bar, I hadn't told Sam about my illness but I felt the vibe that he knew. I was feeling ever so much weaker these days and the fight against cancer was taking its toll on my weakening body, one opponent I knew I could not win. Bang! Bang! Bang! Sam jumped to the floor and instinctively I joined him as the sounds of bullets ricochet above our heads, smashing all of the windows and glasses that filled the bar. It must have been the fire of a machine gun, the amount of mess that was made by it. Mac 10 or 11, who knows, they all sounded the same when bullets were screaming passed your head. I couldn't believe how close to death we were, but in that moment, I felt alive, it must have been the adrenaline hitting me. My hands slightly shook as I pulled my revolver from its holster and let off all six rounds out of the window. "What the fuck are you doing?" Sam shouted as I raised to my seat filling myself a brandy that had survived into a broken glass. I took a sip, carefully watching that I didn't cut my lips and a laugh bolted out of me. "Hahaha! Fuck me! The cheek of these young guns today ay!" Sam looked at me bewildered as we heard the sound of a car volt down the street. I think he knew my mental health was losing all sense of reality as the fact was I was way too entertained by an event that had shaken us. Sam drew his 1911 pistol and raised his arm out towards me. Crash! a brick landed on the floor and skidded towards my feet only metres away, a piece of paper was tied to it. Sam had his pistol aiming straight towards the front door. It was 4am in the morning for fuck sake, we were definitely going to be shut for today now! I walked towards the brick feeling a sense of peace strike me, I know, unbelievable right, but I could feel the energy of Sam's tightly held grip. I tugged at the piece of paper and read the note quietly. "If you're reading this, I guess you're still alive, but don't worry you won't be soon. I'm coming for you, it looks like the chess pieces are in my favour, you have nowhere to hide!" I looked over to Sam with a smug smile. "This next generation are quite creative, what happened to an old-fashioned shoot out?" My eyes were widened, "looks like they beat us to it and made a quicker move, I told you we should have raided one of their houses last night. That was way too close." I felt the adrenaline in my stomach pump and I felt fearless, I was fearless. I thought smart and tried making my next move more strategic to even the odds. I picked up the phone and sat down amongst the glass, "Chris it's me." "Fuck me Henry, you're lighting up the town, bloody Blackpool illuminations, there's that much heat on you. Your mob has been causing a right mess, six houses went up in flames and there is a lot of unanswered questions about to surface, we need to meet." "Meet me at the safe house, it's an absolute mess here." "What?" "Let's just say we've just had some company." "Fuck sake Henry, I'm tired of cleaning up after you." "Well I'm okay, thank you for asking." I smiled sarcastically towards Sam as he listened in on my call. "His name is Kyle by the way." "Kyle Harrison." "That's right Chris, you're the detective." "Right, I'm on my way to the house, be there Henry." I knew Chris had something, I could tell in the tone of his voice, although he did sound concerned. This was good news, off I went to meet Chris. Strange as it sounds I lived for this and I could feel a sense of the old me coming back, as much pain as I was in I almost enjoyed it, the sweet taste of revenge was within my grasp.

CHAPTER 6

Past

On my way to meet Jane I could not stop thinking about all that money on the pool table, my mind was flooding with all possible thoughts of how they made it. It couldn't possibly be all the stall money alone, could it? There was more to it than what I could figure out and I was hungry to learn. I could not wait to learn about the new environment I was getting myself into and being there I could listen in on the conversations. I could smell opportunity lurking and the dopamine in my brain getting released. I was getting a rush so high, I didn't know whether Jane had something to do with it, as I pictured her as a perfect side kick for me. A perfect girl to have under my arm, just like the perfect opportunity I could taste with this Jimmy guy or whoever was around. I just needed to find like-minded people to work with, those who just wanted to earn a fuck load of money so I could buy my own freedom and stop seeing my own go hungry.

I got closer towards my old stall where I had recently been operating from, learning the basics you could say and there stood Jane, so beautiful. Nerves started to strike me, this was a new experience for me, my legs started to slightly shake and butterflies flew around my stomach like I had a field of flowers growing inside me. Now that's got to be one of the silliest metaphors I've ever used to describe how I was feeling, but it was real and that's what mattered. Floating ever so slightly across the ground, moving towards Jane, I smiled. "Hi, Henry, how's your day been?" again, a rush of excitement spiralled around my body, she's 'the one' I thought to myself, before opening my mouth. "Alright Jane, it's been good, thank you. Today's been quite the adventure." "What do you mean?" "Well, you know, seeing new things, new opportunities." "You're quite different, aren't you?" "Yeah, I suppose I am. A good different though, I hope." She laughed but then smiled. I just didn't know what to say, my body had still not settled from the nerves, this was a new one on me. We started walking and talking but I didn't know which way we were going, I was just following her lead. Letting go of control was new to me and I couldn't wait to see what was to happen next, it wasn't like we were on a date, I was simply walking her home. It felt like a date, a first date, as I had never been on one before. I was intrigued and very much attracted to her. As we approached her front door I just wanted to kiss her soft lips, so I did and she was more than happy to reciprocate and it felt so special. I could feel a deep connection between us.

Present

Sam had called Jason to pick us up. "He's here!" I heard Sam call. "Fuck me you lucky bastards, this place looks royally fucked up." Jason spoke with concern as he jumped out of the car to open the passenger seat door for me. "You're right their mate, we are as lucky as a pair of aces." "What are you going to do?" "I'll think of something boy, I guess we got their message though." Jason started the car and asked where we wanted to go. "Saddleworth, I have a nice little safe house up there which will do for now." "Okay Henry, sounds good, we could do with getting out of this place that's for sure." "Don't hold your breath for too long we will be back before you know it." "What time did Chris say he would be there?" Sam leaned over from the front passenger seat and stared deeply at me, I could tell he was still shaken slightly from the whole experience, but he knew as well as me, the consequence of being at war. "He will probably already be at the house by now Sam, you know what he's like, don't worry." "I'm not worried, I'm just getting old. It's been a while since bullets danced above my head and it's normally us doing all the dancing."

CHAPTER 6

I laughed at Sam's wise words and in that moment, we both broke into hysterics. I couldn't believe how old we were, playing in a young man's game. The world had certainly changed and respect had been thrown out of the window. Being the last of our generation, we had to use our experience and all the power we had left in the organisation. I knew as we spoke in the car that this little mobster would be on high alert and no doubt on the run from our associates, as I had given the order. This morning was most likely a retaliation, but the message on the brick, that just made it more personal, a forever reminder of my 'why' behind this pursuit of the mysterious Kyle Harrison. Fucking coward!!

Saddleworth was a pretty place, I would often bring Rebecca up here when she was a child. To be honest with you, I wanted to retire here, it wasn't too long before I was to move into this house. It was just right, big gates and a nice size overlooking a lot of countryside. The journey there brought back some happy memories, I could almost see myself in the fields with Rebecca once again. I knew it was just my imagination visualising the almost forgotten past, I grabbed a tissue from inside my pocket leaning against the window. I wiped the sweat and discreet tears that left my eyes. "Fuck" I whispered to myself, thinking out loud just for a moment as we turned up at my house. Chris' BMW was parked outside the gates, he flashed his lights at our car and I jumped out. The air was so clean, you could taste the freshness on your tongue - something that I was definitely in need of. "Henry," Chris spoke with a serious tone. "Look, this game of cat and mouse is getting out of hand. You're lucky that no civilians have been caught in the crossfire between you and Kyle, do you understand that?" "Save me the bullshit!" "This is for real Henry, I don't know if you realise this but the activity of your firm right now is off the scale and they are leaving lots of tracks that are pointing towards you." "That's why I have you Chris." I grinned and found Chris quite amusing, in all my years I have never cared for the police and in this instance why would I care right now. "Look Chris, just give me what you've got, I don't have time for this right now." "Fuck sake Henry." Chris sneered and pulled out his laptop with some files and CCTV footage. "Here is Rebecca going into the casino in Manchester, but look who comes out with her." Chris zoomed in on the video and showed me a shot of Kyle's face. "Fucking bingo! That cunt is getting it." "There's more Henry," Chris shown me a collection of different files and gave me some inside information. He's got a military background and has been on our radar before, he's a nut case. He got thrown out of the army for crossing the line in extreme circumstances, he's a lunatic Henry, psychotic, like something out of a movie." "Fucking know about that for sure, I figured that myself and that's why he's forever playing mind games with me." "Let me in on it Henry, let me take him out. Imagine what a life he will have behind bars." "No, my brother, he doesn't even deserve any type of life." "Then I know how this is going to end and I don't want anything more to do with this. I've tried with you Henry, to give you a real way out, I'm in the police and I'm damn good at my job. Just let me do what I do best, the right way." "I've been this way all my life, I know what is the right way." I coughed a ball of blood from my throat and spat it into a tissue. "Blood for blood Chris, I think it's time you went on your way." Chris walked off with his head down, but before he went I took some pictures of Kyle on my phone. His hair was short black with a stubble beard and now my imagination visualised him in my mind. All the pain I was going through to strike back at him, fuelled me.

Past

A few months passed by and all I could think about was money and Jane, I had spent all my time after work chasing her around, going on dates, spending what little money I could spare. I was a hustler after

CHAPTER 6

all and I couldn't be spending all the money I had and as much as a womanizer I was, I felt I was becoming a one-woman man. She was the most beautiful thing to me in Manchester. Other lads would take a stare when she would walk by, not when I was around of course, but soon they all came to terms with the fact that she was my girl and I had exactly what I wanted. I was becoming a member of my dad's firm without even realising I was serving an apprenticeship of my own, on the streets and in the bar. I started off being trusted to count the money from jobs they had been successful on, which amazed me as I had never seen the kind of money they were making in my entire life. The money was big and counting it just wasn't in their interest, as long as there was too much to count then they knew there was enough to go around. I'm talking about thousands of pounds here, I was young and that responsibility was unreal. I was my father's son and that's what counted but over time I was getting bored of counting and wanted to start making, even though Jimmy had been paying me a fair wage but nothing exciting like the money they all had. I was still too young in their eyes but I wanted to get in on the heists and whatever else that went on, so badly.

My dad came into the back room where they had me counting the money in piles of thousands. He dropped a leather bag on the table and said "open it", I opened the bag and there laid a big black revolver. "Now son you see this, this is what we live by and in the end, we hope to escape it but this is what we may die by." I stared back at him feeling puzzled and confused and, to be honest, even a slight shake of nerves hit me. "Do you have any questions?" I didn't, other than one thing that popped into my mind. "Can I touch it?" "You touch this gun Henry and you can never go back to being like the others. You're blood - my blood - but once you're in this life there is no going back. I love you son, but this is your choice. You're a man now, age doesn't change that. Trust no one in this world, not even me. Can you live with that?" "But you're my dad." "I am Henry, but you see these walls, you see those at the bar drinking, you see those streets you walk down with your pretty little girlfriend? I own it, we own it and the life owns me, like now it owns you. Every decision you make from pulling this trigger will test you mentally and haunt you from past to present and in return by living this life, if you have what it takes, it will reward you with this" he pointed to the money I was counting and smiled.

Chapter 7

Present

I thought back to the days of when my father brought me into this world, a world that only people with the same upbringing and cut-throat education can be in. Thinking of him in my past situations always supported me, but in this one it was different I had changed and gone soft. With the precious love of my life, Rebecca gone, I remembered my father's words. "This life will own you" I whispered with reflection, knowing the truth to his words only now and he was right, it did own me. It had taken everything away from me and now leading me down this wild goose chase trying to figure out what and why. The Connolly brothers gone and it was me and that fucking Ray left, Ray the driver from the Post Office job. Now my memory has it right that he had written a book about the life, something which I knew was a bad idea and could come back to haunt us. It made me think in realisation that maybe he had mentioned something stupid that could have spiralled all of this out of control. If he wasn't dead already, I will butcher him myself the stupid bastard, I thought biting my tongue.

"SAM!" I shouted, sat in my old chair in the room of my old house.

"I've just had a thought." "Do you remember Ray, the getaway driver??" "Ray… rings a fuckin bell, yeah actually, I do!" "Didn't he write a book, 'Memoirs of a Getaway Driver?' Did you hear about that?" "Yeah, he retired from the game and put it out there. Why?" "I think he must have mentioned some of the jobs we did, because how the fuck does this kid know how we work, he must have linked up with Ray….the fucking bastard. I bet that Kyle cunt is on his way up here as we speak. Ray came here once with the gang after a job that got too heated. We needed to keep a low profile so we all stayed here… Fuck!" I didn't share with Sam what I was actually thinking, it was the fact of what my dad said to me when I was growing up, trust no one and I had broken that rule without realising. The past was definitely catching up with me, to haunt me and paranoia started to rule my mind and my breaths were becoming shorter with the build-up of anxiety. "This place isn't safe! Fuck! They're fucking watching us, I know it. They're out there somewhere, just waiting for us to make a mistake, well fuck them. I've made every mistake in the book. The Chadds were good earners and now they're fucking at my neck. I'll kill every last one of them pricks, I can't believe this!" "CALM THE FUCK DOWN HENRY!" Sam burst his lungs shouting at me as I lost my temper. I felt like what was left of my world was melting around me. I kept having racing thoughts and I could not stop "they're fucking everywhere, those fucking kids. I put food on their plates and every fucking one of them have spat in my face, the fucking rats, all of them. Trust no one, trust no one, he was fucking right, I'd fucked up through being too soft, growing weaker with age." I pulled my gun out in anger and pointed it at Sam, "are you going to fucking betray me too, hey? I've put food on your plate for how many years, how many fucking years?" "Put the gun down Henry, you don't mean this" "How many more people must betray me, your Jason was in control of the Chadds at one point before you ranked him up to us! How do I know I can trust you or him or any fucking body!" Jason ran

CHAPTER 7

into the room confused with all the commotion and pulled his Glock on me.

"What the fuck is going on down here?" "Everything's fine." I heard Sam speak out as I cocked the hammer on my gun. "Fuck off for a minute Jason and put that fuckin gun away." Sam stood with both his hands pointing flat at both of us. "Calm down Henry, I've been telling you all this time that we are going to get this fucker. I feel like I'm constantly repeating myself with you. What don't you get that we are all in this together, we're family, we are all you have left that is just as close to family. What reasons make you believe that I would cross with you? I love you Henry, I've never done you wrong." I looked deep into Sam's eyes and I could hear our hearts beating fast. His face was turning red with blood pressure striking him. "If it wasn't for Jason we would not have been able to get hold of that Spike lad, you know that. Sometimes you're so far at the top of all of this you don't see what's going on at the bottom. You're in your own head Henry and its fucking you up." I gently let my gun hand fall beside me and tears streamed from my face. Jason pulled away with his pistol and stood in shock at the great Henry Slate who was broken. "Don't let him win Henry, this is exactly what Kyle wants, you to destroy yourself." "I hate it when you're right, do you know that Sam?" "Now give me the gun Henry, that's it." I passed over my father's revolver to Sam. He was right, I was just losing the plot and needed to lash out at someone or something, I switched my rage and the room now got the brunt of my emotions. As Jason and Sam walked out of the room I heard Jason whisper to Sam, "fuck me, he's got some demons hasn't he" to which I heard a slap. In that moment, I knew we were more than blood, we were partners in crime, the life that now owned us and was defeating me!

Past

A few years passed and I had become a real man. I was still young, but experience I now had from getting in this exclusive society of criminals, it had rubbed off well on me. I was becoming a rising star in the Manchester Mafia, or so I thought. I had learnt a lot from watching and doing over the years, from being educated on how to plan armed robberies and heists to money laundering and racketeering. There was an expert in the organisation for each type of field and armed robberies were the fasted way to make cash and a lot of it. I was often in the room when planning was taking place and I felt certain I could do it, there was no proper security, every Post Office was a sitting duck. My dad started his career as a bank robber, that's how he got pulled into this world, he then put the money into setting up a few stalls on Market Street and from then on, more businesses, he was smart, a really smart idea in fact. Making your money work for you, most bank robbers and bandits would blow all their money on stupid things, posh watches, smart cars, luxuries, just fucking luxuries. Whereas I had a plan to follow in my father's footsteps and to become number one in what was Jimmy's organisation. I had many chats with Jimmy about moving up, but he always held me back. I didn't know whether it was my dad's wishes, but I knew I had more of what it takes and I didn't understand why I was being held back from moving forward. It frustrated me like hell and with my ambition I started to scope out my own jobs and right now, I was planning one, my first armed robbery. I just needed the right team.

I had been laughing and joking away with a few lads I had grown up with in the bar. Craig and Jamie Connolly, they were brothers and had loose family connections to the organisation I was in. I think they had

CHAPTER 7

an uncle who worked for Jimmy, he wasn't as far up the ranks as me and my dad but everyone had their part and purpose to play. "Alright lads, fancy earning some corn?" I laughed as I approached them playing pool in the vault. "Aww fucking hell, not you" Craig laughed. "Hey, you cheeky bastard, who puts the bread on your table, fucking me." "Yeah, yeah" the lads joked. "So, what do you think of earning some quick cash then boys." "There's nothing quick with you mate" Craig responded as he potted a ball. "Well look, I've got a proposal I want to talk to you about, so what you think. It's a good easy job, I've been scoping it out for a while now." "Where is it?" "Get me a three man team and we will talk." Jamie was too occupied playing his game of pool so I thought I may as well tell them all in full when I had their attention and the team together. "Right boys, I'm off. I've got a few things to sort out so I'll meet you all back here in a week or so yeah. Take care lads and stay out of trouble until next week."

Chapter 8

Now I have known these lads since I started in this place, so I knew they would be willing to graft with me. I went and spoke to my dad to see if I could jump on a job with him, to get some more money saved up. He was slick with his planning and always came away with a load of money. I learnt a lot from watching him, the way he would scope the hits, he loved it. It's what gave him his buzz, even though he didn't have to, as he had money coming in from all over the place: drugs, market businesses, the lot. He was basically an operations manager, running things with grafters on the new party wave but I wanted the thrill of storming into a bank or Post Office and taking that big bag of cash. So easy, so simple, so sweet and this one I had scoped out was a sitting duck. I walked into the private lounge in the bar and shouted to my dad, "Dad, you want a pint?" "Go on then son, get them in." I walked over with the pints in hand and sat at the table. "Hey son, you still shagging that Jane?" "Yeah Dad, you know I've been with her for years now." "Yeah, since you were kids, you little Romeo bastard, you need to spoil her a bit she's a good girl. I'd be on that every night if I was you." "Yeah, well some of us have to work, don't they? Speaking of work, can we talk?" "Yeah, sure." "I was wondering if I could jump on something with you, what do you think? There's a Post Office I've been scoping out that's not been hit yet." "Are you plotting behind my back hey lad, I've told you you're not up for that type of shit. I've told you." "I am ready, I've watched you for years and now is my time to get some of the action." "Do you have money in your pocket each week? Yeah, then shut the fuck up." "I'm sick of you treating me like a dickhead." All I wanted to do was connect with my dad and share in the success of a heist with him, call it a father and son bonding. "Look son, this life owns you, you're already owned and making decisions isn't for you." "What you on about old man? I'm my own man, I own me." My dad started to laugh but then sharply turned his mood. "Do you really? Who puts food on your table, who brought you into this world and put the clothes on your shitty ungrateful back? Me! Now you can go and fuck off and play cowboys with your friends and I swear, if I find out you do a job then guess what, you're on your arse boy." "How else am I meant to move up around here, fuck you old man." My dad raised from his seat and, to be honest with you, I shit myself. I stumbled back but not quick enough and received a punch to my cheek bone. The fucking bastard, if he wasn't my dad I would have knocked him spark out but instead I pushed him back and smiled "You just watch me Dad, I'm taking over this place."

Present

I was itching inside with a feeling that something was going to happen soon. I could feel it in these old bones. I threw a tissue of blood on the floor and headed out of the door. "Sam... Jason, let's go!" "Where we off to Henry." Jason picked up his keys with a stern face looking through me. "Do you feel better now?" "I'm better Sam, let's just move, I can't stand waiting around, time is precious." "Okay," Sam smiled gently. "Good." Before we left the house, I looked around at all the old family photos that were on the wall of the hallway, which led to the door. I picked up a family portrait and brushed my fingers across the dust that slept on top. How happy we were back then as one family unit, to wish for those days once again. I calmed my nerves and wiped the tear from my eye. "If you were only here, I would have told you everything. You would have no doubt hated me and that may have stopped us having our child, but there was a time when you told me to make a choice, to stop becoming the person I am." I spoke directly into the picture as if Jane was talking back to me through the frozen image of a past time. "You would hate me my angel, I was only 16, we were so in love but we did split for a short while through silly stuff and I ended up sleeping with someone else." Sam and Jason stared silently as I spoke aloud to myself. "I am a monster." "Come on Henry lets go for that drive." "All these years I should have told her." "Trust me on this Henry, you did the right thing otherwise you may not have brought Rebecca into the world, you know that." Sam opened the door and we all walked out towards the car. I still had the picture in my hand held firmly. "I just know she will be looking down on me now in shame, both of them." Jason started the engine and drove out of the gates. "Look, man to man, everyone's been there. We spoke about it years ago one night, do you remember?" "I think so! God, I fucked up!" "It was a one-off Henry, don't beat yourself up about it, don't let the past defeat you." "It's coming back to me now, fuck! I think she had a kid you know." "It's not yours Henry, get that out of your head now." "Sam, it might well be you know, another fucking Slate out there, my blood." "Well he will be a man now so just forget about it." In the midst of all the new arrived stress I was experiencing, I received some new photos on my phone from Kyle, it was a picture of the old lady that got shot. I looked deep into the photo and thought to myself had I seen her somewhere before and there it was, I couldn't believe it, all these years how else could I know that face. My brain started doing overtime until the phone rang. "Listen to me you fucking life taker!" "Life taker?" "That's right, you cunt, I'm coming to take yours and all that is left of you.. scum…let's fucking have it. Meet me at the abandoned warehouse in Chadderton and I will end you, you fucking old man." "Listen here you slimy fucking rat, you better come tooled up because I'm going to blow your fucking brains out all onto the floor." I heard him laugh as the phone call ended.

Past

A week had passed and the swelling and bruise on my cheek bone had healed but you could still see an outline of the crack I received, the fucking bastard. I walked in the bar and met with the Connollys and a lad called Ray. He was a driver, a good driver word had it and he had been friends with the Connollys so I thought fuck it, he must be an alright guy. "Alright lads, nice one for coming down. So, the plan is a simple smash and grab, the woman behind the till is an old lady so we shouldn't have any trouble there. All I need from you, is to get yourselves tooled up and make it happen. I roughly estimate about 2-3 grand in the Post Office. It's always busy, so will have to take control if you know what I mean. So, what do you think lads?" "I'm in," Ray spoke first whilst the other two pondered for a moment.

"Are you sure you have this job down," Ray muttered across the table. "Yes, it's all been taken care of, we all just need to play our parts and it will be fine." "How much is our cut?" the eldest Connolly brother Craig smiled, with greed in his eyes. "Equals all the way, a straight split down the middle for us all." Even though I had done most of the work myself, when it came to the score it had to be equal, especially my first job. I needed something for these lads to get excited about, they're grafters at the end of the day looking out for themselves and so was I. Staking out the place and planning all of this was my idea and if I got this right then I know they would want more of the action. As they say, there is no honour amongst thieves and these lads were in this for one thing, quick easy money. Money motivated the lot of them out here and I felt the taste of excitement as we all started to sound like a team. "I'll use a van for the job." "Okay and guns?" "We will sort that out Henry, bring what you have and we will get some muskets." The Connollys always seemed to make me laugh, fucking muskets who do they think they are, but humour aside this was the real deal.

It was a cold brisk morning on the day of the job. I met the Connolly brothers on Market Street where I started out, who would have thought all these years later I'd be the man I am today, all from pinching a little bit here and there. Life certainly is a journey, well adventure I should say and today was my first job I was solely responsible for. This was the day I was to prove myself. I am just as good as the next man. Jimmy gave me a wave, but I didn't speak to him and to be honest it started to play on my mind. Jimmy was like a second dad to me but he too would have stopped me in my tracks, so I had to do what a man's got to do and fend for myself. It's what I'd been doing all my life anyway.

   The walk to our pick-up point was quiet, it was early in the morning and that's just how I liked it. It was a good sign, the sign of a successful start. "Are you ready boys?" "Always! We packed all the gear in the van last night." Craig looked to his brother, "didn't we?" "Sure did Craig." "Good stuff lads, remember we need a clean job, in and out, no fucking about."

The van pulled up on Oldham Road and we all jumped in the back. "OK boys, Billy check all is right with your guns, I don't want any problems, you hear." "They're in working order I checked and greased them up the other day." "Sounds good to me."

   I wiped some sweat off my face before pulling on my bally. It was warm in the back of the van and I could feel my adrenaline pumping as we got closer towards the Post Office. "We're here lads!" Ray shouted. Our conversation went quiet and in that pause of silence I opened the

CHAPTER 8

back door of the van. "Let's fucking have it lads! Let's go! Let's go!" I could feel my lungs expanding, my breathing got faster and faster as we reached the Post Offices entrance!

Present

"Put your fucking foot down Jason, this cunt's having it." My thoughts were still racing of how I recognised that woman but I had to put it to the back of my mind and go to war with a clear head. I couldn't wait to end this cat and mouse chase once and for all. I looked down to the photo on my lap of my family and smiled. "I'm going to do this for all of us." Sam turned his head as I spoke out loud. "I know Henry, we're all in this together, shall I call up some more lads?" "No, fuck it, we will just go, less is more." I watched as Sam turned away looking slightly shaken. He stared at his nephew Jason and put his hand on his shoulder, "if we get through this, you can buy me a drink lad, both of you can." I smiled, "it will be fine." Jason was focused on the road and sat quietly. I could feel an air of excitement just like the old days and the adrenaline filled these battered lungs. I coughed and spat onto the floor of the car as I was out of tissue. Blood stained the carpet of the car, but I didn't care. I stood my shoe on it and pulled out my revolver, "right now lads, I want you on the top of your game, it's going to be a shoot-out for sure, I can feel it in my blood." "Yeah, well it certainly isn't going to be no tea party." Sam laughed amusing himself with his own words. I see him pull off his sawn off and load two shells, along with his 1911 nickel pistol. What a beauty it was, but power is what I liked and I had it sat right here between my hands. "Lock and load boys, we're nearly there."

Jason stopped the car outside the warehouse. I knew it was the one as it was isolated and out of the way from most houses, it was perfect. "I wish we brought back up," Jason whined. He was right though, I should have made the call, but this was personal. This was something only a few of us could do right, too many cars would cause a scene and I didn't want the police turning up, although Chris was always an eye in the sky for me so I texted him. "Chris, I love you mate, I may not always be there for you, like you are for me but there's not a day that goes by where I don't appreciate what you do. Just to let you know the situation is under control and I'll see you when I see you." I whispered the message out to myself, I just had the thought that in this unpredictable situation it was the right thing to do.

I could sense the nervous energy amongst us, it was real and even though we had experience on our side this was a new situation altogether. We were unprepared and in this game preparation meant everything, but what we did have was speed. We had got here pretty quick and even though we were walking into the unknown, walking into a dragon's den, it was all so quiet, like almost no one was here. "It's fucking dark in here!" Jason whispered. "Keep that mouth of yours shut!" Sam shoved Jason forward as we walked quietly up the stairs of each platform the warehouse had. Kyle had left his usual trade mark, on our journey up the stairs, leaving pictures of my daughter stuck to the walls. Mind games, fucking mind games, I thought to myself. I had to just block them out completely. At this point, he had won me psychologically because, for one, we were here and my mind was racing. I squeezed down on the grip of my revolver and pointed it forward as we slowly weaved around each corner of the stairs. We finally reached the top to be welcomed by a group of men standing whilst Kyle sat on a chair. There were five in total and only three of us. I heard Jason cock his pistol to the side of me, I could feel his nerves chewing away inside him as I boldly walked forward with a smile. "I'm glad you could make it!" "And you," I responded. "I've pictured this moment since the second

CHAPTER 8

you took away my gran. Look at you with that antique, who do you think you are, Dirty Harry?" "Listen to me, you fucking cunt, you know what you did, you killed an innocent girl, my daughter and you raped her you sick twisted twat. What man rapes a child? My child." "What man kills an old lady in cold blood? You took more than just my loved one, you took away my life. All of my life I've tracked you down, to now find a weak man. Well guess what, I'm stronger than you and you're fucking out gunned." "Yes, that's true" I laughed. "This kid, hey Sam, what a head fuck! I should just put one in him right now, because I too have been waiting to kill you, from the second you took the one thing away from me that was pure." "Pure?? My gran was pure." Kyle pulled out a picture from his pocket and threw it to me, he had quite the collection. As I looked at them I started to realise where I had known this woman from, the girl I had slept with, it was her mother. I could see her in the eyes of the gran, I looked at a second photo, it was her, "oh fuck, fuck me! What was your mother called?" I walked forward moving closer and closer. "What??" Kyle's face was confused and mine was overwhelmed with emotions. I cocked the hammer on my gun and I wrapped my finger around the trigger and coiled it like a snake. "What's your mother's fucking name?"

Kyle Harrison Prologue

I always thought you were in charge of the decisions you make in life and that fate has a path for us all. You can choose right and you can choose wrong, but when you're a child and you see bad things happen right before your eyes, it stays with you, embedded in your mind.

I was only 6 years old when I witnessed my grandmother get blown away. Before that day I was a good kid and very happy with my life. That day made me more than bitter, it made me a killer and I knew that one day I would put right the wrong they had done. I would be the shaper of my own destiny.

Chapter 9

Present

In life, you only get to live once and it's the decisions you make in between life and death that define who you are. My name is Kyle Harrison, I didn't know all my blood family and the only family I did know, well they ain't here anymore, but my gran has definitely not been forgotten.

I'm sat here looking over Manchester from my luxury flat in Deansgate. Now I haven't forgotten my roots and I have come from some dark places in my life but you would think now I'm here I should be relaxed, well guess what, I'm not. I still rage with anger at my past and the unsolved mysteries that I should have solved long ago. I have spent a life time digging into things but I will get the answers I want and I will get my revenge.

I heard a knock at my door, "Come in Joe," I shouted whilst buttoning my shirt. "Look at you all dressed up, fuck me you look like a posh fucker with that on." "Shut it you! You got them details for us?" Yeah, I hear she's out tonight celebrating or something at the casino." "Good, anyone watching over her?" "No, I need you to get this right Kyle, no fuck ups! This girl is very valuable and could be a good link to the man who fucked your life up. Don't do anything stupid until I find out more." "Nice one Joe! You're like family to me, I appreciate this." "Well don't fuck this up, I got you mate. I'm taking Spike out on a few errands with me so don't worry too much, just keep an eye on this girl, it's a good lead." Now I didn't think too much of this, but me and Joe had been putting together a picture of who ruined my life and over time we have become close. He's like an older brother to me and taught me a lot about this life, that's something you just don't forget. He gave me my first start in this game we play and we've been on some great adventures indeed, but this mission to find out the truth was my last ambition that I had a burning desire for. It was something I had been working towards for a life time and Joe had been getting word off the streets on things and had taken a step back from the gang life to help me on my personal matters. I paid him a fair share for helping me out as I had become leader of the Chadds, which was his little firm. He was still an influential voice and player in the game and most likely had his hands in things that I didn't know about, but still a guardian angel to me, or should I say devil, ha ha. I read something once, I think it was Lucifer who was a devil, I'm surprised it wasn't Joe's second name. He sure was a reckless force not to be messed with, with or without his unknown demons but I had finally tamed him and brought him to my way of thinking. We both managed to come out on top.

"Right bro, I best get going and don't be late tonight, in fact get there early and stake that shit out. I've just sent you a picture of the girl, you've got this, right?" "Yeah, I have, go on then, fuck off mate, I'll see you when I see you." It was about time he went, if he was here any longer he would have eaten me out of house and home, the cheeky bastard. Good lad though, our Joe. The night soon arrived and I sprayed my fresh new aftershave on me. After looking in the mirror at myself and slapping my cheeks a few times, I was ready for the night. I left my flat and headed towards Portland Street, it wasn't too far of a walk to the casino, thankfully. I walked in with a smile. "Lucky night?" the receptionist shouted to me as I walked in and scanned my card. "You know it mate!" I walked down the stairs of the entrance and looked around the place. It had been a while since I had a night out in here and I loved it. All the risk and rewards to be made, but tonight was different I was about to hit a bigger score than the roulette and poker tables could offer, I could feel it in my bones!

I sat there for some time drinking a warm brandy, people watching you could say. I looked at my phone at this girl, she was a beautiful little thing. I scanned my eyes across the entire casino, no girl as beautiful as this one was to be seen. I swivelled my chair to face the bar and downing my drink I instantaneously ordered another one. The burning sensation tickled my throat as I itched my head in confusion. It was getting late, almost 11pm, and I had been sat at this bar a long time. Just as my patience was getting thinner, I noticed a group of girls walk in, laughing and giggling away. There she was, standing out amongst her friends, wearing a black leather skirt and animal printed blouse.

Past

I couldn't bear it anymore, being stuck in this house. The other people who had stayed here irritated me and they were far from family but thankfully I did have one friend, Spike. Now Spike was similar to me, his parents had died in a car crash and since then we shared similar stories and suffered the same yearning of emotions, the loss and separation from the true love of a parent or loved one. We were rough but most importantly we had to be tough to get by in this place. The carers hated us, they would play happy families when social workers were around, but the truth of the situation was, they were only motivated by the money that being a carer could give them. There were now four of us, the other two were only young, aged 6 and 8, brother and sister. They were just what our foster parents wanted, as I soon figured out after hearing conversations that they couldn't have children of their own. That was probably a blessing, due to the way we were treated, who would want them as parents by default, not me. When the children arrived, they were quiet and very anxious. I was around their age when I got put into my first foster home but since then I have had my fair share of moving around. Unlike them I was loud and full of energy, created by a desperate need to get out. I was still scared by the events that happened to me, watching my grandmother die in front of my eyes, it was embedded in my mind without the ease of forgetting. I was a hard child to manage after that and with good reason. All I wanted was to be with my family, anyone who was my own blood, but that wasn't to be. Any last branches of my family tree had separated and moved on with their lives. My gran, she loved and cared for me like no other human. When I think about things now, I had been through such a crazy turn of events. I'd survived two life-threatening situations, a major car collision and an armed robbery. Fucking cunts! Arghhh, I still compressed that pain, but I knew one day I would get my revenge and destroy whoever they were. That I knew for certain and no matter how many years I would spend tracking down those bandits, I would, no word of a lie. I couldn't share this with anyone, this fury I carried with me, I guess this made me who I was. I was only 16 and yet I craved killing so much. Revenge is what I dreamt about at night, behind those masks I would imagine the fear on their faces. Fucking cowards!

CHAPTER 9

We lived in a medium sized semi-detached house, it wasn't very appealing to me, but a bed for the night is a bed and that counts for something for now. Me and Spike, we grew close, but we were fuelled with testosterone and a will to get out of this place. I had made attempts in my past, sleeping rough on the streets of Manchester but I had always been dragged back by the police. There's one thing you learn about sleeping rough and that's the cold nights last a life time. The next attempt would be different, I had been saving money from selling in the school yard. Me and Spike were outcasts, it had always been that way but I knew how to intimidate and between us both we could handle anyone in the school yard. We were always together, inseparable. I failed most of my tests, so an academic future wasn't for me but I favoured history even though I was in the bottom sets. Now there's a subject that you can find a lot of life's lessons in and I once heard that history often repeats itself!

It was late at night and I heard a tap on my bedroom door, it was Spike. My eyes were open from the light that pierced through the side of my door and my mind had not rested. "Are you awake Kyle?" Spike whispered. "You know I am," I replied softly. Spike walked into my room wearing just a pair of black shorts. It was dark which made his body stand out like a silhouette with the slight glare of light shining through the door. He sat on the bottom of my bed and held his hands on his head. "I can't cope in this place any longer." "I know mate, but we will be gone soon." "Let's go tonight, right now." As much as I loved him and as close as we were, his impulsive behaviour did irritate me, but that's why I had to behave like his older brother and tell him to be patient. I could see the light in his eyes as I turned over and rested the side of my head on the pillow. "We can't right now," I yawned. "This is something we're going to have to plan. We will need enough food and money to survive, we can't be living rough again." "Well I can't stay here, this time will be different, I have a plan." I smiled to myself and closed my eyes. "Get some sleep Spike."

The house was now empty while our carers had gone out for the weekly shop. We decided to take the day off school as it was going to be our last, we had nearly finished our time there anyway so what was the point. We had saved around £200 from the hustle and bustle of the school yard, so this was our ticket out of here. "Come on, Kyle, are you ready or what?" Spike shouted from down stairs. I was busy packing my gym bag with clothes and resources. "Yeah mate, just a thought, go and check all the bedrooms and see if you can find any more money." I just realised there must be a stash somewhere in this house, call it petty cash! The carers were taking in a big earn from all of us, the least we could do was take something back for ourselves. I heard Spike run upstairs aiming for our carers' bedroom. The door was locked, crafty bitch. "Fuck sake, it's locked." Spikes eyebrow raised. "Fucking hell, kick it in then!" After a mighty few blows of our feet booting the fuck out of this white door, we heard the lock snap as the hinges fell off the door. "Get in lad!" Spike shouted with an elated smile. I smiled back feeling a small sense of achievement, wiping away some sweat from my face. We started throwing all the wardrobe clothes onto the floor and rummaged like looters. It literally looked like a robbery so at least they could claim on insurance. "Jackpot!" Spike pulled open a compartment of the bedside draw revealing a small jewellery box. Excitement built up inside us both as he opened it slowly. There was a gold watch inside with small gold earrings and cufflinks. We certainly hit the jack pot indeed. I took the watch from Spike and placed it back in the box whilst tucking it into my bag. I looked around the room and laughed, shit, we really did make a shit hole out of this place. Mirrors were smashed which probably wasn't the best idea, as we needed all the luck we could get, but we smiled, we could taste freedom and that had more value than any of the jewellery we found, although it was key to our survival. "Let's go, let's go, we don't know when they will be back." "Okay, calm down, we'll get the bus to town." I thought that we would get into town and pawn that fucking watch and check ourselves in to some cheap hotel and that's exactly what we did.

"£200 you must be mad mate, it's worth at least £350." Spike grew with annoyance inside him as the pawn broker shook his head. "Look mate this is our inheritance, it has a lot of sentimental value, but as you can see we need the money. What's the best you can give us and we'll throw in the cufflinks and ear-rings." The pawn broker looked over our stuff with a magnifying glass and examined it. I knew this guy was trying to take advantage of us due to our age and that's what seemed to be happening. I wasn't daft, I knew a dodgy sod when I came across one, that's why he didn't even ask where this had come from. I can only imagine that he thought we must have stole it, even though we did, but that's not the point. Who was we to judge hey, the old fat bastard! The pawn broker rubbed his chin and spoke in an old thick Mancunian accent. "£275 for the lot, that's my best offer." "Fair enough" I spoke firmly. I suppose it wasn't bad really with what we made in school and off the loot, £475 would last us a little while. We stayed in a run-down hotel in Manchester called Kasha's. It was a room and that was all we needed for now.

Present

She was fucking stunning and I started to over think my approach, I've got this I told myself confidently. How hard can it be, I'll just woo her away with me for the night. She was sat at the roulette table with her friends throwing away money she didn't know how to spend. She was generous though, as I seen her give money to her friends. They were young, about 25 I guess and quite hot to be honest, the lot of them. I could tell they were from South Manchester they just had that snobby, 'we're better than you' vibe about them, but fuck them and fuck them literally the little slags. I walked over to the roulette table and held some chips in my hand. "Red please mate! If you're not red you're dead ay?" I gestured to the girl. "Oh, so you're a Manchester United fan?" "Yeah maybe," I laughed, not giving one fuck about football, but this was my way in. "No more bets please," the staff member of the casino shouted and that was fine with me. Red had always been a lucky colour of mine. "So, what do you do then?" "I'm an actress, what about you?" "Oh wow! I thought you looked familiar what have you been in?" "Well, I mainly do plays at the theatre but I've done a few adverts here and there". "No way, I didn't realise I was in the company of a celebrity!" I joked and seen her face turn. "Cheeky, aren't you?" "I'm Kyle by the way, what's your name?" "Rebecca! Oh, looks like your lucky tonight, you've just won!" "Oh, shit yeah," I split the chips and gave her some whilst taking a proper seat at the table next to her. "I have my own chips thanks, I don't need yours." "Oh, so you're one of those independent women and all that, are you?" She smiled and then responded swiftly, "You know it." "Well I insist, or at least let me get you a drink." I flagged one of the waiters and ordered a bottle of prosecco. "Get me some of your best stuff mate and a drink for all the girls." "So, are you trying to impress me?" "Is it working? You have really pretty eyes by the way." "Maybe, and thank you." This girl was a hard game but I had to be patient, I had to pull her and take her back to mine without causing an alarm. "So, what do you do again, you're so mysterious aren't you?" "I'm an investor, I invest in businesses, pretty boring to be honest, but I'll tell you one thing, maybe tonight I'll invest in you." "Smooth, oh God that was cringe worthy, you are funny."

CHAPTER 9

An hour or two passed, it went so quick but I was running out of time, this girl actually made me feel quite nervous. Being around her beauty was something for sure and believe it or not, after a rocky start we were getting along. I could tell she had begun to take an interest in me and I had won her friends over by buying them all drinks all night, so I made my move, "So, where you going after here?" "Home." "Cool, or you could come back with me tonight." I put my hand on her leg and looked at her with a smile. "Really?? I don't know you." "Aw come on Rebecca, I'll sleep on the couch." "Haha! You're funny." "We could have some more drinks at mine, I live in the flats at Deansgate, you know them big ones, proper nice." "Big ones haha! Well obviously, haha." I see her big smile and honestly, from the vibes, I forgot that I was on a job. I just wanted to take her back to mine and shag her and in the morning just lock her in the flat. Easy work and a free leg over out of it! "Go on then, Mr Mysterious, let's go." She kissed and hugged her friends goodbye and we walked out of the casino together. We jumped a taxi and headed straight to my apartment.

Before you knew it, we were kissing and on it all night long. It was like something out of a porno, this innocent girl had turned wild on me. I couldn't believe it, I certainly had been lucky tonight. Un-be-known to her though, she had just walked into a nightmare, although in this moment I was fulfilling all of her dreams with a penthouse view of the city. I couldn't believe how easy it was after getting a few drinks down her, fucking slag. I just couldn't figure out what part she played in all of this, who she was and how she was connected to my past. It was frustrating trying to figure out who ruined me, but right now I was distracted by the sex and she was getting wilder and wilder, clawing at my back and biting my neck. I threw her onto the bed and there she lay completely naked. I grabbed her by the neck and looked deep into her eyes as I let nature play out its course.

I woke up the next day feeling exhausted, I looked to the side of me and saw Rebecca lying there fast asleep. I would normally wake up early naturally, so I checked my watch, it was 8am. I got up and looked around my flat for Rebecca's phone. I rummaged through her bag and found it there. It was cold, so I threw on some jeans and a top and pocketed the phone. I went to my cupboard and pulled out my Glock and placed it in the back of my jeans, hiding it with my top. I looked at her again sleeping with her blonde hair glowing, she was definitely a 10 out of 10 bird, but I couldn't get too attached, at the end of the day I had work to do. I took her clothes and hung them outside on the balcony of my flat and then quietly closed the balcony door and locked it with the key. I crept outside of my apartment and locked the door, fucking bitch wasn't going nowhere!

I phoned Joe as I walked down the corridor of the apartment and told him the job had been successful. "Alright mate, that's good to hear bro, good work!" "I'll need you to pick us up and is Spike with you?" "Yeah, he's here, I'll put him on." "Alright mate, I'm going to have to crash at yours tonight." "Yeah, no worries bro, just like old times." "Yeah man, sound, just like old times." Me and Spike were like real brothers, we had been hustling together from the start and it was good to see him looking out for himself with some money behind him, although I was always an eye in the sky for him. I was like an older brother I guess, but I couldn't always be there to wipe his arse, he's a man of the world now. I've done more than my part to set him up and I know he does appreciate it and without me he would still be in that foster home haha or locked up. He's not as street savvy as me, I was the brains and he was like, well just like a dog, a man's best friend and loyal companion.

I waited outside at the bottom of my flat, it was just turning 9:30am and I was getting chills through the cold weather. Joe's silver Mercedes

CHAPTER 9

pulled up and the window rolled down with Spike's face smiling. "Get in then you dickhead." "Ay you better watch who you're talking to lad!" "Oh, someone looks happy!" "Are you daft or what, its fucking freezing out here." I jumped in the back of the Mercedes and was curious why there was a positive vibe going on. Joe looked in his rear-view mirror, "we've got some news, well I have some news! I got a lead that can help us uncover what happened long ago. You heard of this book called 'Memoirs of a Getaway Driver?' "No, I haven't?" "Well it's been written by a mutual friend, you could say and in it is the story of a Post Office job going wrong dated back to 1962. He goes by the name Ray and I've set up a meet with him, he thinks it's going to be a pint with a fan." "Well what did it say in the book." "He describes the events you told me, armed up to the teeth and the incident with an old woman." "Fuck that does sound familiar, it's defo worth checking out." "I'm telling you mate, he's one of the guys who killed your gran. Spike pass him the book." Spike leant over to me from his seat and passed me the book, with the pages open to the notes made on that day. I read some of the pages out loud, "it was a regular day, we had everything planned out. I was driving and I was parked outside of the Post Office... I heard a gunshot go off, everyone could hear it, then I saw the lads running from the shop and jumping one by one into the van. I was shitting myself, but the money was great! I remember shouting what the fuck was going on and one of the lads shouted, we had a hero on our hands, an old lady with her grandson. A few days later I read in the paper that some elderly women was shot dead in an armed robbery, but I was so glad the blood wasn't on my hands." I felt my heart skip a beat, I couldn't believe this had been published. I was glad though, but inside I was so angry, the blood was definitely on his hands too, if not more than any of them, the fucking scum bag. He drove them there, into my bloody fate. I can't believe he didn't see that for himself, if you're going to be a criminal, at least fucking own it. Even I knew that, I lived by my actions, even ones

I regret through bursts of anger and rage. "Fuck this guy!" I threw the book back at Spike and pulled out my gun and locked back the slide. "Drive Joe, I've read enough of this shit, let's go." I squeezed the handle of my Glock firm and wiped the sweat from my face, I didn't care what I looked like, I just wanted to kill this mother fucker. "I'm gonna kill this mother fucker, boys!" "Wow don't be pointing that shit at me, trigger finger." Spike's face changed as he saw mine, I was furious. "We can't kill him just like that Kyle, we need to get more information out of the fucker. We need to do this like it's a business." I put the strap away in the front of my jeans and tried to think with a cool head even though my blood was boiling inside.

Past

The night had finally reached us and it had been a long day. Lying on the hotel bed I looked towards Spike and whispered, "we made it mate, this beats the streets hey." "Yeah, but what are we going to do for money?" "Don't worry about that, I have a plan mate but there's one thing certain, I ain't going back there." "I'm not, I don't care if I have to beg, borrow and steal to be my own man." I laughed to myself after hearing Spike's thoughts and it wasn't far from the truth of my plan. After an hour or two, Spike was unconscious and even though the bed was comfy, my ears were alerted to the sounds of a girl screaming.

It must have been a prostitute or something. Being out here was literally survival of the fittest. I crept towards the hotel door and popped my head out. I was stood in my boxers, but literally the curiosity of what was happening overwhelmed me. "Get the fuck out of here, you fucking slag!" It came from a young guy, about 22ish, wearing a white robe.

CHAPTER 9

"Get gone, you whore!" I couldn't help but laugh inside, this shit was comical. The man shouted violently, throwing cash and her clothes onto the hallway floor. I noticed a wallet land on the floor as the woman snatched at her clothes half naked, storming off down the corridor. "He's a rapist!" She glared at me as she walked past my door, I closed it shut and then peered my head out for another look. No way, I thought to myself, the wallet was still there. I ran down the hallway and picked it up, I couldn't believe my luck, I went back into our room and turned on the lamp and opened it up. White powder puffed into the air as a small bag containing what I assumed was coke was in it. Inside was an ID card, it read Joseph Richardson and there was at least £200 in £20 notes, my eyes lit up like the cat that got the cream. This guy sounded really crazy though and he must have caught my eye whilst watching him but this was an opportunity I thought to myself, "Spike get your arse up!" I pulled the covers from him in excitement, "what the fuck are you doing? It's like 3am in the morning." "Look what I found outside," I show him the brown leather wallet that had the imprint of Louis Vuitton on it and explained to him what had just happened. "So that's what all the commotion was?? Jesus, how much is in there?" "At least £200 and a bag of coke." "Fuckin hell mate, that's great, we will last a bit longer out here then?" "I'm giving it back to him." Spikes face looked confused, "why, what we take is ours in it?" "Look mate this is fate, it's an opportunity." "Where on earth did you get that from?" "Who throws money at prostitutes and has these type of drugs and tonnes of money?" "Some old wedged fucker." "Well he wasn't, he was only a bit older than us." "So what, he probably knows a dealer?" "Or he is a dealer!" It took a while for Spike to grasp, which was why I made all the decisions. Anyway, it was already decided, tomorrow morning I'll be going two doors down and handing it back to him.

The morning came and I was feeling the tiredness in my eyes as I walked into the tiny bathroom and jumped into the shower. It felt like it had been a long time since I felt the warmth of hot water. Squeezing the tiny bottles of shampoo on my head, I scrubbed myself before throwing a towel on my back after I felt cleansed by the water. Going through the usual morning routine, I dressed as smart as I could with black jogging bottoms, Nike trainers and a black top...what?? I couldn't afford to dress to impress, in reality! I laughed to myself, but I was sure going to try. At the end of the day it wasn't about the clothes, it was the respect and the relationship I wanted to build. I knew life was all about knowing the right people to get ahead of the game, but this was my move and I had to play it bang on, I needed to impress. First impressions go a long way they say. Bang, bang. I knocked on his door around 12 midday. I felt nervous inside and my excitement had died down but I could smell opportunity. The door didn't open for about five minutes, as I waited a slight rise of anxiety kicked in. Should I just leave it on the floor and go, one of my thoughts suggested. No, I ignored myself, this is the right time. I looked behind me and clocked Spike repeating my actions of last night, watching what was about to unfold. I heard the sound of the handle squeak, it was him. "Who the fuck are you and what are you banging on my door for?" The man I knew as Joe from his ID raised his arm out widely, leaning against his door. I knew he was a rough streetwise lad, just at first glance. His short hair was close to a skin head and his face just looked well lived in. I could only imagine he had seen and done a lot.

I looked at Joe square in the eye before opening my mouth, "I found this last night and I think it belongs to you." I coughed into my hand clearing my throat, his eyes looked me up and down before he made his next words. "Oh right, nice one our kid." I passed over the wallet and he took it from my hands and took a good look inside. I see him smile then he looked back at me, "everything seems in order, how old

CHAPTER 9

are you anyway?" "16 mate." Joe held out the bag of coke and offered it to me, "do you want some?" he laughed. "I'm good mate." "That's a good answer." He turned to the room and walked inside, "come in youngen." I followed him inside as I heard him snort some of the coke from the bag and yawned. "This will wake me up." He turned again and looked at me whilst counting the money in his hands, "it's all there, what's your name kid?" "Kyle," I responded. "Well Kyle, when I was your age I would have just took all this for myself. 200 fuckin pounds is a lot for a youngen like you." He counted £60 with his fingers and passed it to me. "Well take this as my appreciation." "Thanks Mr Richardson." Joe started laughing to himself once again. "You know what kid, I like you, call me Joe." "Okay Joe, I'm going to cut to the chase, I need work, can me and my brother work for you?" Joe paused for a beat, I could tell he was shocked by the whole situation that had arrived at his door step. "Well what's your story kid?" I took a deep breath and started to tell, "well, my parents died so my gran cared for me as a child then an unfortunate turn of events happened in a Post Office hold up and she was killed, shot dead in cold blood. Since then I've jumped from foster home to foster home until my brother and I, by default, decided to break away from it all. Look Joe I know we've only just met but I need this opportunity!" There was a silence between us as I spoke with a sense of urgency.

"You don't hold back do you kid, fuck me that sounds like a movie." Joe laughed out loud and shook his head. "I'll do anything mate." "I definitely get the feeling you will. I'll take a chance on you kid, but do you really know what you're getting into because once you work for me there's no going back." "That's exactly what I wanted to hear," I put out my hand and shook his. "Welcome to my world mate." I could tell from the off he liked me and my first impression had paid off. I knew he was taking a gamble on me, but that I could assure him would pay off tenfold. This guy had just gained two new workers, working for peanuts probably, but still it was our survival. I shouted Spike and he came walking into the room, I knew he was just outside on the corridor listening in to the conversation. "This is Spike, where I go he goes." "Alright mate, welcome aboard." Spike looked slightly tense and nervous, his confidence was a little deflated in the new environment and world we found ourselves in, following my decision.

Present

I was still furious and the car journey felt like a life time, as we were on our way to meet this shit head going by the name of Ray. I bet he was an old fucker, a 'wannabe' big time Charlie, soft cunt, fuck him. "This guy is going to get one big fucking surprise, trust me lads." We arrived outside a bar on Oldham Road called The Cotton Tree. We parked up at the back and just sat in Joe's car for a moment. I was curious to meet this man, although I was fuming I was intrigued too. I could feel my heart pounding as I was about to exit the car. "Right now Kyle, let's not have too many fireworks go off, we need to keep a low profile." "Okay," I responded gritting my teeth. All I could think about was blowing this mother fuckers head right off, but Joe was right, he had the information I needed to make my next move. I had to try and calm my nerves and stop the adrenaline pumping to keep professional and to keep my word, because even though I was ruthless, it's your word that is all you got in this life.

I walked into the bar and for some reason it didn't feel right, I felt on edge but that just may have been me over thinking things. This was just going to be a conversation and a meaningful one. One of those

CHAPTER 9

conversations that would be resolved by just a few words and settled over a pint. It was still early and that explained why the bar was so quiet, there were only a few people inside which did make the situation perfect and in all, quite intimate. Me and the lads got a drink at the bar and walked over to an elderly man who looked around 60, he may have been older but I didn't care. This fucker was partly responsible for my gran's death, so why be so kind to old eyes hey? I took the book from Spike's hands and placed it on the table in front of him.

"So, Ray, I guess this is our first meet." He smiled and put his hand out to shake mine, then looked at Joe and realized this was not the kind of chat he was expecting. I could see it in his wrinkled face, as I did not shake his hand. "Indeed, it is." "I've heard a lot about you." "Yeah, well, all I hear about you is this book, you really don't know me, Ray, but I know something about you." "And what's that youngen?" "Don't call me a fucking youngen, you piece of shit." "Manners boy, manners." This fucker was irritating me to fuck, if we weren't in a public place I would have just killed this cunt already. "Are you taking the piss, I think you know why you're here, why we set this up?" I picked up the book and tore out the pages and shoved them in his pint. "Now you think that was clever do you?" Who the fuck did this old fart think he was, talking so calmly to me like I was a child. I spoke stern and looked at him square in the face with my eyes wide. "Read it! Does this not remind you of anything hey?" "Yes, the book I written." "Well, let me tell you a story Ray, some things you missed in your fucking book. 'There once was a child who was happy and loved and then some stupid fucking idiots went and killed his only loved one, the boy's grandmother. She was around your age when the boy last seen her.' Now do you want to tell me who the fuck took this little boy's loved one or what?" "Ah... I see, so you were the child?" I launched my hands over the table and gripped Ray by the collar. "Now you better tell me and stop playing fucking games, alright??"

I shoved him back into his seat and pulled my gun out and placed it pointing under the table. Ray seen a glimpse of me putting the gun under the table and the air in the room started to change. Now I loved my gran and I would do anything for her and this was one of them moments where I knew she was looking down on me disappointedly maybe, but still with a warm smile on her face that I was doing something right in her honour. I could feel my finger wrap around the trigger and my instincts were telling me to shoot, just fucking shoot. I could hear my thoughts repeat over and over again in my head. Fuck! I thought to myself, I needed to get myself together really quickly and get what I needed. "Joe, you bastard, I can't believe you've put me in this position," Ray spoke with anger in his throat. "Hey, eyes on me!" I spoke firm holding my own with the cocky bastard. "It's just business, nothing personal Ray," Joe sniggered. "You bastard," Ray shouted. I quickly scanned my eyes across the room as Ray had broken the silence in the bar. "Look, you old fat, cunt, if you don't give me the names of who did the job with you I promise you now you won't see another day anytime soon." "Why so you can shoot me straight after, fuck that for a game of soldiers." "You don't have a choice mate, you give me the names on that napkin right now or those grandkids of yours won't be visiting you this Christmas. So, if you want to see the light of day, you'll do exactly what I'm saying to you, right now." I stared deep into his eyes as I watched him pull out a Parker pen from his jacket pocket and write down the names of those who were on the job with him all those years ago. "If you don't kill me, they will!" "Well that's just something you have to decide for yourself isn't it. I'm good to my word and you will live to fight another day, you mard arsed bastard." Ray slid over a napkin with the names on it. "Now you best not be fucking me about Ray because you know I will fucking kill you".

CHAPTER 9

I looked down to the napkin and read the names out loud, "Jamie Connolly, Craig Connolly and Henry Slate." I was shocked to see Henry Slate's name on the list, this guy was a big heavy, a fucking don you could say and he was on the fucking list. I was shocked as the Chadds had been linked with his organisation for years. I kept my cool and dug for more information. "Anyone else I should know about?" "That's it!" "Well, where can I find these Connolly fuckers?" Ray gasped the words out quietly, "The Tavern Pub in town, they drink there every day." I slowly pulled my gun away and watched his face as he sold out his friends to me. I pulled out a £20 note and placed it on the table. "Get yourself a drink on me, old man." "Kindest regards Ray," Joe smiled nodding his head. "Two more things, who killed my gran and who organised the whole heist?" I could see Ray's face turn red with blood pressure, he muttered and stumbled on his words, "it was the Connolly brothers who killed your gran and Henry orchestrated the whole thing!" "It's been a pleasure, old man," I joked as we left the table feeling a greater sense of purpose and achievement. All my life had come down to these moments of finally knowing the truth.

Past

After a few days had passed of being under the influence of Joe, he really exposed us to the life I had only dreamed of. Hitting private parties on the roof tops of hotels, getting in all of the clubs we had long waited to experience. These were the days, but little did I know this was far from the icing on the cake. It was also good to see Spike enjoying himself as we both definitely deserved it, coming from the past that we once lived was no luxury. Joe paid for all of our drinks and offered us the usual street drugs we would help him sell, but that shit wasn't for us, the money kept us afloat but I knew my time was coming to prove myself on a bigger level.

"Get some of this down you lads, you'll be on it all night!" Joe smiled letting the toilet door close behind him. "I'd rather sell this shit, money's, money." "You're right there mate but I just want you to have a good time." I pulled a smile and looked back at Joe, "do you see me smiling," I laughed to myself, "then I'm having a good time then." Joe patted me on the shoulder. "You're a good earn and a good lad, go and get yourself a drink." I passed the money to Spike and told him to get us one. "Listen Joe, I know it's not been long and you've been good to me and Spike, teaching us the ways of the world, but I want to get some action. I've got a job lined up that I'm in the process of working out in my head." "You intrigue me lad, go on." "Well, you know like it's the Queen's Jubilee coming up this week, I want to take advantage of it. All of the shops will be shutting up early and there's just one I have my eye on." "What shop? Small shops don't have big earns mate, it's petty shit that, go for the big ones lad." "It will be a stepping stone for me and a chance to prove to you what I can do." "This sounds interesting, so what shop is it." I hesitated in telling him all the facts because I didn't want to feel discouraged, but I knew I could do it. "Fucking easy mate, it's a pawn shop full of money mate and gold watches. I've seen it with my own two eyes, I pawned one not long ago and, to be honest, I want it back as the cunt ripped me off." I could tell Joe's ears were listening as he finished another line of coke, he was literally off his tits. He turned and looked at me with a deep stare and shook his head. "Well, if there's anything you need just let me know and I'll hook you up." "Thanks Joe, I appreciate it mate. Have you got a bally and a tool I could lend?" "You want a shooter? Mate that's for the big leagues!" Joe raised his top ever so slightly that shown the glimpse of a pistol tucked into his jeans. "I suppose we have a similar relationship to you and Spike, where I go, she goes." Joe laughed! I didn't seem the slightest bit surprised even though I had only seen guns in the movies, but there was no issue at all, it is what it is, protection at the end of the day. "So, we good then,

CHAPTER 9

you don't mind me doing this." "Course not, just don't get your arse fucking caught, I own you." "Fuck off !!" I laughed. "Me get caught? You're mad mate and yeah, of course I work for you." "You know it," Joe scraped his fingers through his short hair and pushed open the toilet door. "Come on mate, let's get you a woman. When I was your age I was always in and out of the brass houses." "Do you have to pay?" "Do you fuck, you just pick one you like and that's it, you're in, everyone here knows me and that means one day they will know you too. This is what I like to call my kingdom, right here. I own this place and you're a part of the Chadds now and that's almost better than being famous. You're going to be a somebody kid, just like me." I felt humbled by Joe's compliments, but a stream of nerves hit me. I had never been with a girl never mind a woman. We walked over to a table where I saw a few elders and a couple of women sat at a table. "Here's your drink bro," Spike appeared and passed me my drink. "Thanks mate." We followed behind Joe and sat amongst them whilst the music in the club played loud and the lights shined.

"These are my boys," Joe shouted loudly with a proud smile upon his face. He put his arms around us both and nodded to a woman besides us, "Caroline, this is Kyle, my youngen, he's a good one this lad." The women were half dressed wearing seductive clothes. Man!! I was feeling the vibe, I took a large swig of my drink and smiled. "You alright love?" "He's a cute one isn't he," she replied. I felt a little bit embarrassed and God knows how Spike was feeling, I suppose he was in his own little world. Joe pulled some money out of his pocket and shoved it in the woman's bra. "See to it that he has a good night, you know what I mean Caroline." She laughed and then smiled at me. "Come on you." I had only just met this woman and I couldn't believe my luck. She pulled me by the arm onto the dance floor and started swaying her hips against mine. I got a huge hard on and I was ready to go at any minute. All I was thinking about was what I wanted to happen. After time had passed and she became bored by the music we walked into a room at the back of the club for VIPs. There was a bouncer standing outside the door and I felt slightly intimidated by his muscular figure. He was big, and I mean fucking big. He would have killed me in one punch and that's the truth! "Who the fuck are you?" The bouncer questioned me as I looked up to his face. I couldn't show any fear so I did what I thought was best. "I'm fucking Kyle, Joe's fucking youngen." I pointed to the far table referencing where I had come from. "Oh, I've heard about you, you better watch who you speak to with that attitude, go on, get in." 'Fucking prick, what was all that about?' I thought to myself, 'no need.' The room was lit dimly and there were couches in every corner. This woman I now knew as Caroline started to kiss me and caress my body. This was a school boy's dream and I was fucking living it. It was the first time of the night that I was genuinely enjoying myself. I had worked hard all night grafting for Joe, passing bags and collecting payment. I guess this was his way of saying thank you.

The next morning my head was fucking banging from all the drink I had. Somehow, I had arrived at my hotel room without any memory of arriving here. I heard someone in the bathroom using the shower and even though my head was fucked, I felt at peace. I pulled myself out of bed and sat leaning over, "Caroline!" I shouted at the bathroom door. "Who the fuck's Caroline?" Spike walked into the room with a towel wrapped around him. "Fucking hell mate, I didn't realise you were here." "Fucking hell, I thought that bird was still here." "Mate she didn't come back with you. Fucking one of Joe's boys brought you back, you were hammered mate. You came in here and was flat out, gone mate, in seconds." "Fuck me, really? I thought I was pretty sober you know." "Anyway, what happened when I was gone?" "Never mind that! What happened with you and that woman." "Mate, it was unreal pal, it's way up there with one of the best nights of my life." "No way, I swear man I've got to give someone like her a go." "Mate you will do! Trust me!" I pulled my bag out from underneath my bed and started to throw some clothes on. "Hey man, coming out here's been the best decision I think we've made." "I know mate! Speaking of decisions, I'm on the verge of making one this week, the Queen's Jubilee." "What you mean mate?" "Well I was talking to Joe last night and I'm going to rob that old, fat cunt who mugged us off at the pawn shop. "Fuck off!!" Spike looked shocked as he dried himself down. "How you going to manage that?" "Well with it being the Queen's Jubilee all the shops will be shutting early and the police will be way too busy to even think of responding to a robbery. We can then just get off and disappear into the crowds, our hotel is only two minutes away too." "You don't have to do this one with us, if you don't want to mate." "No of course I will, we stick together man, ride or die." I laughed at the last few words, 'ride or die'. I don't know where he got this shit from but it did make me smile. "Alright mate, what I'm going to do is pick some stuff up from Joe and then tomorrow we'll get it done, but first, go and make us a drink of water mate." I got up and walked into the bathroom with some speed and threw up what was inside of me. Swilling the toilet with a few flushes, I felt a small sense of relief.

After leaving a mess in the bathroom I headed back to bed and started strategizing what my plan would be, but I couldn't concentrate with this shit hangover. I did what was best and tried to get some sleep after drinking a pint of water. A couple of hours passed that only seemed like minutes and before I knew it, I was knocking on Joe's door. I heard the latch on the lock open so I walked in, "shitting hell man put that shit down!" Joe pointed his M9 pistol at me, his eyes were red and clearly hadn't come down off the whizz. "Close the fucking door!" I didn't feel afraid at all, I don't think it hit me that he was stood there holding a loaded gun at my face. I closed the door and looked him in the eye. "Wild night hey Joe?" "Yeah! WILD FUCKING NIGHT!" Joe lowered his shaking hand that held the gun. "You shouldn't sneak up on a man like that, you just don't fucking know, you know." There was coke all over the place, the place was a mess. The result of another great night I assumed, but Joe had clearly let himself go this night and mustn't have had any sleep at all, I could tell from his eyes. Joe placed the gun on the table and sat down on the couch, I followed him and sat down beside him. "I thought I'd come and pick up some stuff for my job tomorrow, I need something that can take somebody out easy." Joe leant over to the table and picked up his gun, he emptied the magazine from the handle and slid it back inside. "What about this? I can get you a piece, it's easy." Joe ejected the magazine once again and pulled back the slide on the pistol. Pointing it to his head he started to mumble, "this is easy!" Joe whispered, "one gentle squeeze and BANG! It's all over." I heard the gun click as he pulled the trigger and smiled with a sinister tone. "I can imagine!" I responded, only imagining what shit Joe had seen and done for him to get so crazy about killing. I suppose we shared the same instincts, like two puzzle pieces that matched. But I only wanted a quick fix not a kill, as there was only those who I really wanted to hurt that I wanted to un-wrath my anger on. "Here, caress it, feel it, hold it like it's a woman in your hand." Joe placed the pistol in my hands and I could feel the real weight of it. This was the first time I had held a gun before, but it felt right. Something inside of me ignited and I could understand Joe's obsession of the power it held after looking down the sights and imagining taking out who ever made that day in my past happen. I placed the gun back on the table. Joe threw one of his famous smiles and spoke with affliction "Now that power boy, quick and easy! Remember these words, it's not how many you kill, it's who you kill." He was right, I had dreamed of killing those involved in my grandmother's murder and the best way to get revenge

CHAPTER 9

one day was being very selective. "Joe, I need something that packs a punch, something that can knock a man out easily." "Okay, I have just the thing." "Oh yeah and two Bailey's." Joe stood up from the couch and walked to the wardrobe in his room, he bent down and grabbed a leather bag. He paced back towards me and threw the bag at me, "have a look in there and take what you fancy." Inside this bag was full of soft weapons from knuckle dusters, police coshes, small bats, big fucking knives and a set of gloves and a few balaclavas. "Is it alright if I take these?" "Yeah mate, sure, why not hey! You remind me of when I was on my first job, I can see the excitement in your face." "We'll see what happens hey Joe, I'm pretty confident it will all run smooth." "Hey, you best not forget my share." "Course not!" "I'm just testing you," Joe brushed his hand across my hair. "I take it you had a good night then?" "Yeah it was brilliant, I best get off though mate and thanks for the stuff, I appreciate it mate." "Hey, no worries our kid and next time you can pay for Caroline yourself!" Joe sniggered as I walked towards the door.

Chapter 10

Present

A few days passed and I couldn't stop thinking about the names on that napkin, I was filled with joy and shock at the same time. I was sleeping on the couch of Spike's apartment and it kind of reminded me of the old days and just like the old days I was thinking of our next move. I felt relaxed and one hundred percent focused, I just wanted to let my emotions run wild as I could feel my heart skipping beats.

I sat there quietly in my own little world and then my thoughts started to race. I could not believe I had been working and paying my share to the man who ruined my life all those years ago. Honestly, I was shocked but grateful at the same time because I knew how he operated and it was time for fate to take my side. Henry Slate was now a dead man, his rank and his position could not save him. I did not care or empathise one bit and I was going to make his life a living hell for however long it takes to put that man in the ground. Actions have consequences, even I know that after all my own wrong doings, but I had age and some wisdom on my side, they would never see me coming. I was one rotten egg in his organisation and I planned to crack and make as much mess as I could along the way. There was nothing I could not do now, I had

CHAPTER 10

the names, I knew where they lurked and I was going to get my revenge. You may be thinking he didn't take the shot but I still hold this fucker accountable, as they say, a captain must go down with his ship and if it wasn't for his bright idea of doing the job in the first place then my beloved gran would have been around longer. The fucking amateur scum.

Thinking of the man made me furious and I had a lot to think about with the time I had on my hands as I waited for Joe to arrive. Spike hadn't come out of his room and it was coming up to 11am, after a few days of being here I picked up on his routine. I still saw him as a big kid really, he never changed, always the same old Spike, "Spike!" I shouted in an attempt to get his attention, the lazy bastard. "Oi dickhead! Wake up and get ready! Joe will be here soon, he's just text me, we have work to do." "Alright mate! Five more minutes and I'll be up." "Fuck your five minutes, he will be here then, get your arse up." "Alright, fuck me, you forgetting whose flat this is mate, it's fucking mine." I laughed to myself at his response as he had momentarily forgot who the real gaffer was. "Who put money on your table to get this place, you cheeky bastard? Me, so get your arse ready and in here." Cheeky bastard still tried taking liberties with me but what can I say, I love that kid - he's my brother from another mother, literally. "SPIKE!" "Jesus mate, fuck me what's with the shouting?" "Joe's text, he's on his way up, go and let him in, he will be here in a minute." I lay back, still in a deep thought with myself, pondering ideas in my head. I was curious to see what was new, Joe knew everything that was going on in the streets, I could not run the Chadds without him. He was my eyes and ears, but I was the full skeleton that held this shit together but he was too valuable and secretive with it. "Yes boys, what's going on?" Joe walked through the door with a spark of energy to him. "You good, Kyle?" "Yeah, I'm just thinking mate, we need to make some moves fast and start taking action, I can't sit in here any longer. All these thoughts are running around in my head, it's driving me nuts, I feel like a lion in a cage!" "Then let's let that beast of yours out then, what would you have me do?" "Kill that old fuck Ray, I can't have him running his mouth off on the streets." "Agreed, I will get Spike to handle it." "Ah yeah, right, nice one! I'll sort that old cunt out, but you should have just shot him there and then," Spike responded throwing on his leather jacket. "Can you handle this Spike? I've got a lot on my mind right now and I need to get to the Connolly brothers fast." "Everything will be fine, I'll find that old fart and they won't see us coming we're still under the radar." "Right, I'll leave that with you then Spike, text me when you have new info, go on lad get to it." Spike threw me the keys to his apartment and made his way out, "don't forget to lock my fucking door!" "Spike, take some lads with you if you need too." Joe spoke sternly.

"So, what are you thinking Joe, what do you think we should do?" Joe's eyes gazed at the floor for a few seconds and there was a small silence between us, just for a moment before he opened his mouth.

"Well, word on the street is Henry's daughter didn't come home a few days ago and he is worried, like any father would be. There's something I have got to tell you Kyle, I had my suspicions that it's the girl in your apartment." Joe spoke with a glimmer in his eye. "Fuck off, it's not... is it?" "You did all of this for me?" "We're like blood Kyle, I've got your back." "Fuck me, you ruthless bastard!" "You think he would suspect it's you who set this up?" "Fuck him, I want the top spot, we will kill them off soon." "They're a big firm." "I've been busy Kyle, we're on the rise, it's time for us to take our place," Joe spoke with excitement, like a big kid on Christmas Day. "You fucking know it!" I felt so excited and couldn't believe my luck, Joe was a guardian angel after all. I was filled with questions about how he knew it was her and how he got

CHAPTER 10

close enough to find out how it was going to go down, but we had work to do and there was no time to sit discussing Joe's work. All I could say was he done good and now I was going to make things interesting, really fucking interesting. I could feel my dark side erupting, spiralling out of control inside of me. Let's fucking have it, I thought, the silly little bitch isn't going to know what's hit her.

"Well you threw a right curve ball at me there our kid, I didn't expect that!" "Well I just thought it would have been useful." "But how did you know Henry was involved?" "I've been in his world for a long time, I've seen all the people he associates with from time to time and after asking him how he started out he pointed to them. Over time, just like you, I put the dots together and the book was the icing on the cake," his eyebrow raised but I was happy with him, all the money I had paid him over the years had finally paid off. "I'm just letting you know now Kyle, that when we fuck these old timers off, I'm running things from the top and you can be my number two." "Sounds good to me mate, all I give a fuck about is getting what is mine and my revenge. The fucking scum, I almost nearly looked up to him and his accomplishments." "Well it's a good job you have me, we're our own men."

I could feel it in my bones that I was going to do what was right by me, I pulled out Rebecca's phone and showed it to Joe. "I'm going to fuck Henry's head right up with this, no word of a lie, this cunt deserves it." I looked down to the phone and I see multiple missed calls from him. I smiled to myself like a street cat, "let's fucking have it Joe, it's time to make a move. Drop me off at my flat mate." "Okay, but what are you going to do." "You don't need to know on this one, just make sure you're around for a few hours, I might need you."

Past

The next day soon came and I had talked over the plan with Spike. We chose our weapons and was ready to go. Hooded up in dark clothes we walked towards the pawn shop, it was midday and I was feeling pumped full of energy and excitement. I emptied my big gym bag before coming out and the day was running as I imagined. Standing at the side of the door to the pawn shop we pulled our balaclavas down, as we wore them as bobby hats to blend in, but once they were down it was show time. I pressed on the buzzer on the shop door and the door opened. This was it, there was no going back and we had to step up to behaving like professionals. This was it, our chance, our golden opportunity as well as taking back what was ours. I barged the door open and swung Joe's cosh straight across the old, fat cunts head before he could even open his mouth to say, 'what the hell', Bang! My first blow struck him hard, followed by a metal fist off Spike. The old, fat cunt fell to the floor and I swear I heard him squeal. I swung open my bag and smashed the glass cabinets filling the bag with all the watches and jewellery that was on show. I saw the watch we had pawned and threw it in the bag. "Where's the fucking money?" Spike started shouting at the top of his voice, blood was pouring all over the floor. His nose was bleeding and swelling had appeared from the man's eyes, he was painted in colours of black and blue, it was disgusting to be honest, but we had to do what had to be done. This was the beginning of our rise through the ranks. I opened up the till and took all the notes that were on show. 'Fuck it,' I thought 'we've got enough.' So I shouted to Spike, "it's time to get the fuck out of here," but before I made my leap to the door I gave a kick to the old, fat bastard's body. I could hear him squealing like a fucking pig waiting to be slaughtered. It made me laugh though as it wasn't far from the truth for him. We royally fucked this guy up big time.

CHAPTER 10

"Come on Spike, leave him now, we've got to go." "Take that, you fat, ugly cunt! Did you really think you could fuck with us, fuck you!" Spike spat at him as we left the shop. "Come on, fucking leg it!" We ran down Market Street taking some back street detours to our hotel. "Pull your bally up," I shouted across to Spike. He listened, as I pulled mine up, back into a bobby hat. "Come on! Go! Go! Go! We're nearly there." I could feel the jewels in my bag jiggering, I hoped they were not going to get too damaged. "Come on, straight through the doors. Right, chill now, we've got to be cool." We walked into the elevator of our hotel and as soon as the doors closed I felt the highest sense of 'fuck me!' I couldn't believe it; the adrenaline was so addictive and the smell of success was the only drug I needed. I didn't know much about all of that jewellery shit but I'm sure Joe would, he's into all that shit. We banged that hard so many times on Joe's door that he must have thought it was the police. "It's us! It's Kyle and Spike." We both shouted over lapping each other. I heard the twist of the door knob open and Joe was standing there in his famous white robe. "Fuck me boys, come in, Jesus you're both sweating like fuck, I guess today was the day then." "Yeah, it sure was." Spike's eyebrows raised.

I placed the gym bag on the table in the centre of the room feeling a sense of accomplishment, joy and success all ravelled into one. I wiped the sweat from my face and, joining the bag on the table, I threw my balaclava and placed the cosh. I knew Joe was just as intrigued as us to count up what we had just made and see the loot. I knew Joe loved this kind of shit and to be honest I was warming to it too. "Come on then, get it open." Joe spoke firmly with his eager eyes. I unzipped the bag and there it was, gold watches, silver watches. Some good names in there too but I didn't care for trend, money is all it was to me, a means to an end. Whichever way you looked at it, you couldn't fall in love with treasures like these, it was best to be sold on and forgotten about without a trace. "Fuck me, this must be about six grand's worth of gear in here, easy." Joe reacted filled with excitement. "So, you reckon you could get rid of this for us." I looked through the bag and picked out the gold watch we had previously pawned, it was a nice one, a men's Rotary. "I'm going to keep this one as a reminder of where we have come from, the fucking rotten pigs." "We might as well sell it with the rest of them, those people were wankers." Spike spoke thinking of the one thing I had taught him, money is money. "You could take a pick of one of these bro, smart gear in here mate." "Nah, I don't want no trace, it's best to be long gone and sold and we need the cash anyway. How long do you reckon it will take to get rid of all this shit?" "Give me a week or two and I'll flog it all but remember what I take is mine, my cut. Do you understand that?" "Yeah of course." Me and Spike nodded. I dug my hand into the bag and searched around for the cash I took from the till, there was just under £500. I gave Joe £250 straight up. "Thanks for the tools mate, take this as another part of the cut." I kept the other £250 for me and Spike. "Hey what the fuck man, where's my bit." I could see Spike was alarmed, but I reassured him. "What's mine is yours, remember that. We stick together, all of us." I addressed Joe and he smiled. "This is very kind of you Kyle." "It's fine mate, no problem at all." "You two have certainly made your mark, a pawn shop, you clever little bastards." Joe's grin raised even wider. "I think it's time I introduced you both to what I'm a part of, so you can see what this shit's really all about." I felt my heart beat more rapidly as he spoke. I knew there was more to what we had already seen and I felt so ready, so determined to learn everything that I needed to know. How to stay ahead, how to come out on top and how to become a man of power.

CHAPTER 10

Present

We set off to my apartment in Joe's car, I was racing with excitement but I kept it under control. This was the perfect opportunity for me to make a statement, for all the pain Henry had caused me in my life, I was going to royally fuck him up. He thought he was retired and made it to the end, well I was going to show him the end of my gun one day very soon. The day was coming and as the minutes passed and we got closer to my apartment I could smell revenge in the air. I stepped out of the car outside my apartment block and popped my head in the crack of the door looking direct at Joe. "Just make sure you're around when I call," he nodded and drove off quickly as I slammed the door.

The tension in my heart was inciting as I made my way up the lift to my apartment. Each step I made towards the door of my room was treaded carefully and quietly as I hoped she would be asleep. I cranked my key in the door and opened it slowly. I walked in and she was lay there wrapped up in the bed sheets. She had royally made a mess of my apartment and smashed the place to pieces. "Fucking bitch," I spoke quietly to myself. I pulled my phone out, sticking it on record and placed it on my kitchen side table. I crept towards her as she slept, I lay myself down next to her body and smelled her hair as my head rested on the pillow next to hers. She instantly woke and started screaming, hitting me with her hands. I grabbed her by the neck and started throwing her around, wrestling with her on the bed. I pulled the blanket away from her and undone my jean buttons, I started fucking her, she cried for help and screamed out loud, but I was far stronger than she could ever be. "Why have you done this to me?" she screamed. I just laughed to myself as she trembled in despair. "You deserve this, you fucking slut!" "Get off me!" she screamed slapping me as hard as she could, I caught her hands and pinned her down laying all my weight on top of her. With one hand, I pulled out her phone from my back pocket, she snatched it off me screaming. "You don't know who I am do you? My dad is going to kill you!" I kept pounding away and punched her in the ribs, she screamed with tears streaming down her face. "Go on, call your fucking dad!" I looked at her and it was surreal I couldn't believe I had Henry's child by the neck. She dialled the phone screaming away and shouting for help. "Shut the fuck up! No one can hear you!" I pulled out my pistol from the back of my jeans and pushed it straight into her head then slowly moved it into her mouth.

You could see the fear in her face and the bruising from my fist, the blood from her nose dribbled onto my Glock. It was like something out of a horror movie, I felt like Freddie Kruger and that thought gave me an idea. She screamed for help down the phone. "Daddy help me," she cried. I heard Henry on the opposite side of the phone going off his head panicking like a bitch. I'll give him something to cry about, the fucking pussy. I gripped the handle of the Glock firmly, smiled at Rebecca and pulled the trigger, BANG!! Blood and brains sprayed everywhere on the pillow and bedsheets. I felt the warmth of the blood hit my face and I shouted down the phone "You're next!" I pressed the end button on the phone and looked at the body pulling myself away. She was still warm and I felt the adrenaline in my body pound. I got up and wiped my face, I could still smell her scent in the air. I knew I had done the right thing, taking one of his own away from him like he did to me all those years ago. It was a shame she was young and pretty, but it had to be done, even though it may have been seen as a waste. I walked into the kitchen and thought I'd leave more of a message to make it personal, I grabbed a knife and did some art work on her body, leaving the date 1962. I had the whole incident recorded on my phone ready to use at a later date along with pictures. I picked up Rebecca's

CHAPTER 10

phone and wiped the blood from it and stuck it in my pocket.

Past

A few weeks passed and we were learning on the job, running drugs all around Manchester, travelling everywhere up and down the country. I had never seen so much money floating around in cars. The big news on the inner circles was that Pablo Escobar, the biggest drug lord in Columbia, was holding a ridiculous percentage of the world's cocaine business, something along the lines of 80 percent. It blew my mind how all of this shit was being sent all over the world and being carried in the back of our boot. The purest and finest shit that any drug user could take. It was shit and the punters had no clue, other than it kept them up all night talking shit. I was enjoying life but still my nightmares would creep in, it was only last night I woke up trembling like a bitch over the flashes of seeing my gran being killed. Bang! Bang! Bang! Yep, I could hear those gunshots every night when I closed my eyes. It motivated me and kept me sharp but I was burning inside with a foolish killer desire. We were in Joe's motor on our way back from a drop off, it had been a long day, I looked behind my seat and saw Spike flat out in the back. "£20k hey mate, not a bad day at all. I know we took a high risk but that connect was worth it. See mate, life's all about the risks you take, the necessary ones like today. The only reason I took you along is because I wanted you to see the real deal. You can't learn this shit by thinking about it, you've got to be about it and remember, only take trust on the word of people you know inside out. There can be snakes in this game." "You know a while back, when you said it's not how many you kill, it's who you kill." "Yeah, vaguely." Joe winded his window down and exhaled smoke from a cigarette, as some ash fell onto his designer shirt. "Well there's something I've not really spoke about and maybe you could advise me." "What on?" Joe interrupted. "Killing someone." "Who?" Joe spoke calmly but raised an eyebrow. "I don't know who it is, but the fuckers from my past who killed my gran, she was all I had mate and it burns inside me every day. It's always at the back of my mind and when I meet people like who we met today, it makes me think, could it have been someone like him. You know, it's hard to point a finger when you don't know who this fucker is, but I need to do something about it. I think maybe in a few years I'll join the army or something and get some real fucking killing experience." "I get you mate, I have lost too, but the army mate, that's meant to be some tough shit. Waking up early doing all that exercise," Joe laughed. "You see mate, I don't care how big they are, they're not going to stop these bullets ha ha. No one is bullet proof!" "True mate, I know I've got it in me mate, I could fucking do it. I know exactly how I'd bring pain to whoever this fucker is." "Well mate, revenge is sweet but you're only young mate and as much as it must kill you inside, you've got to be patient. Like you said it could be anybody, I'll try my best to help you narrow it all down." "Thanks Joe, I appreciate it mate." "There's a meeting tonight with everyone, all of the Manchester gangs that are in control at the top. There's been some shit going on, some London faces have been trying it on with our lot. I think you'll learn something, so you can come with me, but word of fucking warning, don't speak out." "Thanks Joe, I appreciate it mate." Fucking hell, I had only been in this world two minutes and it had me totally consumed, I couldn't believe my luck. A proper sit down with Manchester's biggest heavies even though I was less than a fucking grain of sand in this whole circle. I could feel the momentum in my journey, I had seen shit that a lot of people my age would never imagined, it gave me the edge over all I believed.

CHAPTER 10

We arrived at a pub just outside of Manchester. It was a Sunday and the streets were quiet, other than the amount of cars that were parked up and these were smart cars too. We stepped inside and the pub was booming with people, all dressed sharp and tooled up for certain. I sensed the vibe in the room and there was definitely no scope for anyone joking around. We were here on a serious matter that had troubled the one and only biggest Manchester firm. Even though there were other gangs here, that we would normally be competing with, we all followed the same code and paid the same price to the top. When situations like this would arise, small conflicts between gangsters from separate gangs would be put on pause and the first and most important thing would come first and that was that this was a business, a whole operation, where every pawn was affected in this game of chess. Joe introduced me to some of the well-known and respected faces, but I did as I was told and just nodded and shook hands with people. We had to be on our best behaviour as we were representing Joe and the Chadds. Although he was the leader of this gang, the real power and connections came from above. He was a charismatic leader, a straight up street playboy who was liked by most of the elders, simply because he must have reminded them of their past youth.

"You see them over there, Kyle?" "Yeah," I replied. "That's Henry Slate, he's a very important player here, he runs things. There isn't anything he doesn't know. To the right of him is Sam, his right hand, a little bit like who you will become under my wing. Feared just like the lot of them." I held a straight face and nodded. "Well it sounds like this really is a serious matter." I reacted to Joe's reply, catching Spike staring into space. "Stop fucking staring Spike!" "Sorry mate." 'Clumsy bastard,' I thought to myself, 'this was not the place to stare.' At the end of the day they were all fucking killers, men of real power and what were we? Just kids.

Everyone started to slowly crowd around this Henry Slate character, leaving a few paces in front of him. The room went silent as he started to talk and everyone's ears perked up. "Right everyone, I'm sure you have all become aware of why I've called you all in today and the rumours on the street you have heard are true. Our conflicts with some London faces have escalated, but we will not stand for this, we are fucking Manchester at the end of the day and that makes me Mr fucking Manchester to all of you, because I run this shit and no London cunt is going to take what is mine, which in return is yours." Fuck me, you couldn't hear a pin drop. This Henry guy certainly had some influence as the room was so still. "There is word that they will be trying all kinds of shit to cause us all pain. I've heard that the Jones twins, Collin and Rob, are going to send their crew down here. So, just like our generation before us, we will meet with them and with no doubt in my mind, they will be right back on that fucking train, back to London, fucking Cockney bastards. They think they can bully us around, not a fucking chance, we're not stupid cunts." Everyone in the room was pissed off by the thoughts of the Jones twins trying to take a piece of our world. I understood that business happened in every city and I knew that first hand but trying to take over a whole city was unknown to Manchester. You could see why this Henry guy was going off his rocker at the situation. If I was him, I'd happily just kill both of them fuckers, live to fear no man. Joe had once mentioned the Jones brothers to me on a car journey and from what I gathered they were nothing more than posers who hanged around with stupid celebrities who wanted to taste what it was like to be in the presence of so-called dangerous men. Yeah, they had done well taking over London, I have my respect there, it's a big city, but trying to take Manchester's underworld scene, what a load of bollocks! "Right that's all I have to say, feel free to stick around for a drink, if not fuck off, but we will act right now. For those of you I've mentioned, get yourselves down to the train station, I want

CHAPTER 10

to know exactly when they arrive, understood? It should be some point this week!"

Chapter 11

Present

I went back into the kitchen to get some bin bags whilst wiping the blood off my pistol on a tea towel. I wrapped the bin bags around the body before rolling her up in the sheets and blanket. I didn't have long before people would have become alerted by the gunshot, so I rang Joe. "Mate where are you, I need you down here now. Shit's just got real." "Okay mate, I'm coming, I'm two minutes away." "Come straight to the apartment mate."

I sat down on my couch for a moment and looked at the body wrapped up in the covers. I had to get this place cleaned up, the apartment wasn't even in my name but I didn't want anything coming back on me. I couldn't have the police sniffing around, and when you're a man like Henry I'm sure you have a few crooked cops under your belt, but a man like him would no doubt want to handle the situation himself. I sent some photos over to Rebecca's phone and sent him a text message. "I'm going to fucking kill you!" I then rang his phone out of curiosity to see how he would react. All I heard was "I'm going to fucking end you!" I laughed and put the phone down. I couldn't believe what I had just achieved after all my life I had been waiting for these moments of

CHAPTER 11

revenge and it tasted sweet, even though I was only halfway through my mission. I heard a knock at the door and let Joe in. "What the fuck did you do?" His face looked shocked but I think he was more shocked at the mess of the house than the body that was wrapped up on the bed. "I had to shoot the bitch Joe, an eye for an eye. But don't worry mate, I had some fun first." "You sick bastard, you." I laughed losing my composure but I quickly regained it as I looked around the room. Reality hit me and I started talking straight, "he got what he deserved Joe and I'm going for him after the Connolly brothers, I'll save the best till last, plus it gives me more time to fuck with his head. You'll never guess what I've got on this phone." I paused for a moment after speaking quite quickly and finished my train of thought. "So, we need to get this shit cleaned up fast."

"I'll make the calls for a clean-up." "Wait…we need to move this body ourselves." "Tape up the blanket then with black tape so she doesn't fall out and we'll carry her to the car boot." "Sound!!"

For a small girl she was heavy, carrying her into the lift with Joe just looked like we were moving a tonne of bedding. We taped her up pretty good and fortunately for us no one was in the corridors. It was quiet, just the way I liked it, but I couldn't believe how quick the smell started to fill the air of her dead body. This was the longest I had been around one. Joe parked his car close to the lift of the flats and we quickly slammed her body into the boot of his car. She didn't fit right away, so we had to put the back seats down. "You better not get her blood on my fucking seats!" Joe slapped me on the back as we got in the car. "Don't be daft, I used bin liners, her full body is wrapped in plastic." "Right! Good fucking job you crank." "What??" "You heard me mate, you're the only sick fucker I know who would fuck the bird then kill her after it." "And you're the only fucker I know who is going to help me out with it.

When you think about it, her death is on your hands as well." "Yeah, I suppose, another notch on the bed post hey" Joe laughed and quickly pulled out of the parking space.

"So, what plan you got then?" I scratched my head and wiped the sweat from my face. "We need to dump this body, I'm thinking an old run-down warehouse or something. You know of any?" "Yeah, I know the perfect one, leave it with me." "So, what do you want to do about the Connolly brothers?" "Torture the cunts, one of them pulled the trigger on my gran, so they're getting well and truly fucked up. But I want you to do something for me first. I want you to take this video I'm going to send you and have one of the boys set it up, on a loop, on the TV in that scruffy old house we use in Ancoats, the fucking drug den." "Oh god, you filmed the full thing, Jesus!! Good job all he can see is your behind, you're lucky he can't see your face." "Yeah I know! That's why I filmed it from a distance." "You should have done a balaclava job." "I know, it was kind of sloppy to be fair."

My mind started running away with me, but oddly I didn't feel guilty that I had just taken a life, I actually felt empowered and productive that the tables had turned. I didn't care what the world thought of me, I was a gangster and a fucking good one, the little boy in me had died a long time ago. I started plotting in my head, ways I could fuck with Henry's head. I knew in this game of chess I already had the upper hand and he had no idea who I was and how the hell I was making moves so deadly. I wanted him to experience all the pain I had felt for all these years. I wanted to get in his head so he couldn't think straight and I'm sure to God it was working.

A day passed and word was out that Henry's daughter had died. We had her strung up in the warehouse of Joe's choice and we were back on the road. A meeting had been called by the organisation, but were

CHAPTER 11

we going? Were we fuck!! We had business to take care of, not public appearances at the enemy's bar. Fuck that, our business was with the Connolly brothers. Now I heard these were hard cases back in the day, so me and Joe were both tooled up. We were staking out the Tavern Bar where they drank, we waited outside in the car. Two old men walked into the bar after about half an hour that fitted the description, one was wearing a black Crombie and the other was wearing a leather jacket. These old timers had charisma about them, you could just tell from the way they walked and looked that there was something different about them. It didn't scare me, not at all, I was fully loaded and ready to pop some fucking shots. My Glock still had some blood stains on it that had dried onto the steel, but I didn't mind, it gave it a nice finish. "Are you ready then?" "I'm always ready Joe, you know that." I smiled as my blood began to rush around my body, I had no time for nerves there were two of us and two of them, we had youth on our side and we were strapped up. I was going to have to get creative on this one.

Joe opened the glove compartment and pulled out two balaclavas and a Beretta M9 pistol. "We'll use these, there are cameras in there." "Sounds good." We threw on the gear, all pumped up raring to go, locked and loaded. It was a good job Joe had changed his car to a Range Rover as we needed the space in the back. Taking out two people was going to be a challenge, but none the less we had this under control. "Let's fucking have it!!" I yelled out loud, getting myself pumped up. We ran into the bar, guns blazing, letting off a few warning shots. "Everyone get on the fucking floor," I barked to all the punters, to which I seen the Connolly brothers sat there in an ignorant bliss. "Everybody stay calm, we're not here for the fucking money, we're here for those two, Jamie and Craig Connolly, get your arses up!" The bartenders were shaken and the other casual drinkers were lying on the floor as expected. "No one needs to be a hero for these two cunts, do they?" I shouted to the others in the bar as I walked straight towards them, holding my gun to their heads. "Who the fuck are you two pair of clowns, do you know who you're fucking with??" Jamie Connolly reacted, showing no fear in his face. "I'm your worst fucking nightmare, you old cunt. Now get the fuck up!" "Fucking shoot me, go on big man, pull the trigger!" Craig spat on the floor. "Joe grab that cunt, that's music to my ears you old bastard, just you wait, you don't have a fucking clue that your time has come."

Past

Some people started to leave the bar, I could tell how serious the whole situation was and I felt the burning desire in me again, wanting to prove myself valuable. "Joe, why don't we head down to London right now and just fucking do something about this." "We can't do shit without the go ahead from Henry. That's just how it is Kyle, you've got to be careful of the ripples the stone makes once you throw it in the water." "What the fucks all that about." "Someone once said the same thing to me when I was your age. You're young Kyle and being naive is all a part of your youth, but this is big man shit, where experienced leaders like Henry call the shots. You see him over there, that's Sam the Knife, now you can only imagine how he got that name and that group of men there, well that's the Connolly brothers with Ray Smith. They built everything you see around us with Henry's knowledge and the influence that his father gave him. Some would say 'is it a blessing or a curse' what these situations create for people like the Jones twins. What I'm trying to say to you mate is that there are foundations that have been built. You have to honour that and respect it, it takes generations to build an organisation like this. That's what keeps the Manchester

CHAPTER 11

Mafia so strong and why we can't just go all guns blazing in these circumstances, without the nod of approval or else you'll be dead too. It's who we represent mate, you're a part of something big now and we each have our role to play, that's just how it is." Fuck me, I didn't even realise, what Joe was saying was the truth and I feel like I had only just understood it all. He was a part of something big and that meant that I too was part of something big. It was like a big family, something I didn't think I'd experience in such a short time and now my life began to grow with purpose. It was more than trying to break through the ranks, it was more than just money and the lifestyle, it was the pure loyalty between everyone in the room, but not to say that everyone was as tightly favoured to each other as I'm sure that some skulduggery did happen from time to time. In my heart though, this all now meant something and I was fortunate to be a part of it.

"I see Joe, I see," I replied. "I'd introduce you to a few people but I can see they're busy with business." "I know, there's a time and a place for everything." We walked towards the exit of the bar and bumped into one of Joe's friends. "Alright Jamie?" he uttered as he bumped into him. "Alright Joe and who are these two new faces?" "They're with me." "I know that, otherwise I'd have pulled my shooter on them." Jamie winked at me and smiled at Joe. "To be young again hey, these little bastards haven't seen nothing." "Well, they've seen more than I did at their age." "Listen Joe, a word mate." Joe walked to the side with his back turned to us and started talking with this Jamie guy. I wasn't deaf and I could easily overhear what was said. "There's something I need you to do for me, but first, be careful who you bring into here, this isn't a fucking youth club. This was a private meeting!" "I know, I've told you they're with me. They're a part of the Chadds and good fucking earners, young and wanting to prove their worth." "Right, well you know where we stand with this kind of shit, Henry wants your full attention this week so whatever you have planned put that shit on hold. You can see we are on high fucking alert, look at him." Jamie pointed with his eyes, in one sharp stare towards Henry. "He's stressed out of his fucking nut and I know you're a straight shooter, so I want you to help resolve this situation." "You know I'm here to play my part Jamie, but don't take this the wrong way, I don't take fucking orders from you, only Henry." I could feel the tension at the end of Joe's words. "You cheeky little bastard." There was a pause between the two, Jamie was a lot older than Joe, but it was like watching two lions in the room having a face off, even though they played for the same team. A distinctive laugh bolted from Jamie's throat, "you youngens!! The balls on you!! The fucking balls!!"

Present

In a way, it was humbling to see that these men were showing no fear, but I was about to knock that last bit of courage right out of them. Seeing myself in these two was something I did not expect, the fearlessness in their eyes was like looking at my own reflection, but I had to break them, "get your arses up, you're coming with us." "Pull the fucking trigger!" "I fucking will, you dickhead." Bang! I let a shot off next to his ear, it dazed him. "Fuck me Jamie, we've got ourselves some cowboy gangsters." "Fuck me, you cunt! My fucking ears!" Jamie screeched out loud. That certainly got things moving, we dragged the two old fuckers stumbling left to right outside the pub. "Get a fucking move on now," I shouted aggressively flexing my muscles and pushing them towards the car. "Get the fucking boot open Joe." "Rookie mistake their lad." Craig laughed to himself, so I pistol whipped him hard across his face. "Rookie? You old bastard, you know what, fuck you, you don't

CHAPTER 11

have a clue what's coming." The boot swung open and I pulled the trigger again, aiming at the old fucker's knees. "Ahh! Ahh! You fucking bastards! Ahhh!" Squealing was all I heard from that fucker's mouth when I emptied one into him. I pushed him into the boot along with his brother who was also asking for, so I twatted him over the head with my pistol just as I had done with his brother. They may have been hard cases but you couldn't take away the fact that we had the power and they were about to learn that. Bang! I fired another slug into Craig's leg. They were screaming and shouting like little bitches. Music to my fucking ears I thought, these fuckers had it coming and I could justify it all in seconds. One of these cunts had pulled the trigger on my gran and I would not spare a second thought in putting one in the chamber of these pair of clowns. "You won't be running off anywhere soon with them legs," I shouted slamming the boot door on them. "Fuck me!" Joe smiled, "I didn't expect that, where did that come from?"

"I don't know Joe but it's done now and these fuckers know we are for real." "Let's just hope they don't die of blood loss before we get them out." "Don't be daft, it's a fucking flesh wound." "No, it's not Kyle, it's a knee cap." "Same thing!" We both jumped in the front seat and could still hear the sounds of them wailing and whining in the back. 'So much for hard men', I thought.

After an hour of driving to an isolated abandoned mill, we parked up in the car park. It was dark and out of sight so we opened the boot and watched them wiggle like worms. I pulled off my balaclava and shown my face, "listen here you fucking dickheads, my name is Kyle Harrison, does my name mean anything to you?" "No," they both mumbled. "Well it fucking should." Joe passed me a silencer for my pistol as I watched their faces look up to the stars in hope they would get out alive, but there was no hope for them as I had made up my mind and it was clear.

"What do you both want, money? We can give you money, just name the price." Jamie tried to negotiate even on his last legs and I could see Joe's eyebrows raise in consideration, but I was the one deciding their fate, I had been waiting so long to find out my true grandmother's murderer. "It's not about money, it's about revenge. Fucking revenge! Do you get that, you fucking idiots? Does 1962 ring any bells with you? The past has finally caught up with you. So, which one of you killed an old woman in a Post Office job back in 1962?" Lay in the boot they both stared back at me in shock and disbelief. "Who are you?" Craig spoke, gritting his teeth in pain.

"I'm that child you stared at, with no remorse, as you took away my grandmother. The only person I had in my life that was there for me." I felt myself become a little teary eyed as this was an emotional moment that I did not expect. "It was me!" Jamie blurted. "No, it wasn't, you fucking idiot, it was me!" Craig shouted aggressively over Jamie's voice. "Which one of you did it? There can only be one of you who pulled the fucking trigger. I was there, remember!" "You will live to never fucking know which one of us did it, you cunt," Craig yelled pushing himself forward to the opening of the boot. The cheeky cunt launched himself forward with a strike aimed towards me with his fists. My instincts moved me back as he fell forward onto the ground. I drew my pistol towards his head as Jamie screamed and shouted. I kicked Craig multiple times in the stomach and I felt my heart beat faster and faster as the life was leaving him. I leant over him on one knee whilst still holding my gun to his head. "Is that all you have to say, are you done now hero?" Blood dripped from his mouth as I squeezed ever so gently on the trigger. A muffled popping noise of the silencer erupted to blood splattering all over the floor.

I pointed my gun towards Jamie as tears streamed down his face in

CHAPTER 11

horror and regret. "Get him by the legs Joe, we're pulling this cunt out." "Get off me you fuckers! You have no idea what you've just done." I could tell he was shaken by my actions but nothing was saving this fucker. I pulled my gun towards his head then hesitated for a moment as I decided to push the barrel into his flesh wound. I got off on hearing him cry out in terror, there was something so contagious about it, that I had missed. This reminded me of my war days, when I killed a man with my bare hands. "Now…it's Jamie, isn't it? That's right, fucking nod! Listen Jamie did you pull the trigger? I promise you, if you don't tell me, I will pull the fucking trigger!" He was shaken still, in a trance like state and whimpered and mumbled to himself like the weak, old man he was. I paused for a moment and reflected on the fact that one of these fuckers, if not this wanker, had destroyed all I knew and I watched flashbacks in my mind of my gran falling and bleeding out on the floor, like the fate of this man's brother beside me. It gripped me, as I could see the pictures in my mind, so I did what was necessary. I put my gun in the mouth of Jamie, "listen to me you no good cunt." I could hear him mumbling on the barrel as I looked him directly in the eyes. I could tell his life was flashing before him as his eyes streamed. "You may have been the man of your day, but I'm the man of today. So, you better take that with you to the grave, you ugly cunt. You took all I had, you and that twat of a brother so now it's time for you to go." With my free hand, I held his hand firm and slid his finger to the trigger. "Go on, do it, fucking join him! Do it!" He put up a weak fight in the attempt to spare himself a few more seconds as he choked on my barrel as another muffled popping sound went off. The Connolly brothers were dead, I felt a sense of achievement like I had just won a gold medal. All these years wondering who it was, I guess I'll never know now, but I had my inklings, not that it mattered now, they were both dead. Henry Slate was the one to get the full force of my actions, as he had orchestrated the full operation and I held him responsible for the true death of my gran. If it wasn't for him, I would not have been on this wild goose chase all my life.

Past

I saw the big man, Henry, walk towards Jamie and Joe, he opened his hand from a clenched fist and shook Joe's hand. "It's good to see you pal, I've heard good things, good things Joe. I can see you're mentoring those little bastards, but remember where your responsibilities lie, I need you to make sure these Jones brothers get brought to me, don't fail me." I knew this was a big ask for Joe, but fuck me, Henry Slate personally asking Joe. He had a full fucking army and out of all the people, he chose Joe. I knew there was more to it and I could feel it in the air. I knew Joe well, but this was a tough one, the whole organisation was involved and this was a big part to play. "Okay Henry," Joe nodded and turned towards the door. I could tell from the drop of sweat that dripped down his face that this was going to affect him. We got inside his motor and started to drive. "Open the glove compartment." I opened it and passed a bag of coke to him, it was the only thing in there other than a magazine cartridge for his pistol. Joe dug his finger inside the plastic bag of coke and sniffed long and hard with one hand still on the stirring wheel. "FUCK!" Joe said under his breath. I felt a lot of tension and I was slightly intimidated to talk. I hadn't seen Joe like this before, I didn't know whether the pressure of the situation hit him or whether there was something else on his agenda that he hadn't told me about. To be fair, we were quite open with each other, that's how the best partnerships are, aren't they? I plucked up the courage to speak, "what's wrong Joe?" Joe sighed and exhaled, "I knew that something was on the boil tonight. I've got deals that I'm going to have to put off now for fuck sake! A lot of money to be wasted! Fucking Londoners fucking with my shit." "You've got this mate, you know I've got your back." "This is man shit Kyle, you're just a boy." "Fuck you Joe." I snapped instantly at that comment, it pissed me right off. I was sick of being looked at as a fucking kid. "I might not be old and fucking wrinkly like them cunts in there, but I know my shit, I know how to get things done. Stop fucking worrying and stressing man, you're a professional. We will just kidnap the fuckers when they turn up at Manchester." "It's not that easy, you cheeky little shit." "Well we will just make it easy wont we? Think about how much respect you will get if this comes through." "You don't get it, this is the Jones brothers. I won't get out of this, if this doesn't work out, if you fuck up, you get fucked up." "Shit, well then we've got to make it work."

A few days passed and the pressure was starting to build up more intensely, I could see that Joe was on the urge of a breakdown if we didn't come up with an idea fast. So, I too was thinking long and hard. We got a phone number to the Jones' home addresses in London through some connections of Joe's, and we were deciding what action to take next. "Joe, I still think we should just kidnap these fuckers but maybe do it methodically." "What do you mean?" "Well, say we arrange to pick them up from the train station in a nice car and say that Henry would like to meet to discuss this new business arrangement. We could just say he agrees with the terms but wants to disclose things personally as he wishes to build a relationship with them. It's that personal touch that these two Jones twins couldn't refuse." "They would be armed though and they would check us out." "Let them, all we have to do is play along and make them feel reassured." "They would have protection with them too." "Then we will just get two cars?" "I'll think about it." "What's there to think about Joe, we're running out of time, we need to start taking action right now." It was true, we did, the clock was ticking and all we had done was discuss without making any calls. "Okay," Joe ran his hand across his head and stared at the number on the table, he picked it up and counted the digits with his eyes. "I'll call them this afternoon, I'll have to let Henry know the plan so he can approve it."

Joe was gone a couple of hours and I was sat in his apartment thinking to myself. Is this really it, you do or die, the world I'm now in! Fuck me, I never realised the reality of the situation, we had to make this work I told myself. If it all fucks up, it was me at the end of the day who suggested it, me and my big fucking ideas. I should have just kept my mouth shut, Jesus. I could feel self-doubt creeping in and there I was just sitting there whilst everything was in motion. I felt helpless that I couldn't do anything, but at least I was the brains of the operation. I laughed to myself, stroking my ego, patiently waiting for the news to see if Henry had approved it and all of the right calls had been made. I can't lie, this shit was exciting, watching your ideas spring to life from your head to reality, there was nothing more satisfying. It was strange though, with all this excitement and pressure going on, spending time by myself brought up some bad feelings inside me. It was that reminder that I'm actually making no progress in resolving my own personal situations. I know it was still early days and the journey I was now on had proved to become quite the distraction, but I did need Joe's help. As soon as things cool down I'll be back on it, but again, we couldn't fuck up because no doubt I would suffer the same consequence as Joe and I had Spike to look out for. For fuck sake, he wasn't the sharpest tool in the box, but when let loose definitely a potential weapon. There was a knock at the door and I leaped from the couch. "Alright Kyle mate, what the fucks going on pal." It was Spike, speaking of the devil. "I'm just waiting for the phone to ring. I was just thinking of you mate." "Oh right, I was thinking Kyle, I want to get into boxing." "That's not a bad idea mate, it will do you good." "Thanks mate, you never know you could be looking at the champion of the world right here." I laughed admiring that he had a dream, but I snapped back into reality when I heard Joe's landline ring. "Shit, the phone." I leaped over the couch and snatched the phone off its hook. "Hello." "It's Joe mate, I won't be long now pal but the plan is in motion. Henry has sent a message across, an invitation. He's going to have a sit down with them, that's all I know so far. I've got the cars sorted, how does two Bentleys sound?" "Wow, sounds great mate!" "They're going to be coming down tomorrow, so no fucking about." "Course not mate." "Alright mate, see you soon."

Present

Half my job was done, I still had to find Henry Slate and put an end to him, the mother fucker. I could feel my hatred build up inside as I thought about him. The true cause of my pain. I told Joe to get creative so we strung the bodies up inside the mill. I took some photos and sent them to Henry, 'you're fucking next' I typed out on his daughter's phone. I knew he would be losing his mind at this point, which is what I wanted. I felt like I had the whole situation in the palm of my hands, but I wanted to make things more interesting and cause some more disruption. I had a lot of thinking to do before I planned my next move.

I couldn't believe how close I was to achieving my goal, my mind was cycling at 100mph, so I thought it would be a great idea to relieve some stress and shake things up a little. "Joe don't worry about this mess, your car I mean, don't worry about it mate, I'll buy you a new one after all of this comes to an end." "Well you fucking better, blood stains, it doesn't come out you know." "Well we're going to have to get rid of this car at some point." "Can you get your hands on a Mac 10, we need some fire power?" I looked at his face and knew he couldn't believe the words that had just come out of my mouth, after we had only just got rid of the Connolly brothers. "What for, we already have our pistols?" "I know, but I want something more explosive, can you sort us out or not?" "I know a guy who will sort us out, I'll make the calls."

It felt a bit quiet without Spike being on this adventure with us and I hadn't heard from him for a few days. I was beginning to worry about the kid, but I couldn't let the thoughts of him consume me as I had to keep my head clear. I tried calling him while Joe was busy on the phone but still I had no answer. He will be fine, I thought to myself, he's a grown man and a reliable one. I just hoped the job I had given him wasn't too overwhelming for him. I looked at Rebecca's phone and sent a text message to Henry, 'you will soon get what's coming to you! I know your daughter loved every second of it' I typed quickly and tried to think of every possible way I could psychologically get in his head.

"Right, it's all good, my contact came through, it's going to be about 3k for some sub machine guns." "We're good for it, don't worry about the money." "I'm never worried about money, you know me." "What's it for this, anyway?" "I'm thinking we should create some disturbances, that's what I'm thinking and nothing beats chaos than causing a load of noise." "Right! Sounds good." Joe looked in his rear-view mirror and could see all the mess in the back of his car that was left. I knew he was fuming inside, so I pulled out a bag of coke and let him take the first sniff of it. He loved this car and I had made a mess off it, it was the least I could do. "Fuck me, where have you been hiding that?" "I always carry a stash on me, you know me, I run out of energy sometimes and need a boost." Joe pulled out one of his keys and sniffed up hard. "You can't beat it, this stuff is quality, Escobar shit." Joe started laughing and snorting. "Escobar shit! You funny bastard, this is street shit!" "Yeah,

CHAPTER 11

well, it all starts somewhere, you taught me that." "I'm proud of you mate." Joe put on his leather gloves and put his gun back in the glove compartment. "I remember when you were a kid. I never thought you would get this far, you've done me proud lad." I felt my heart beat fast as Joe confessed his feelings and I never expected to hear him say that. This was a first for me, I had always looked up to Joe and now he was right by my side, going through all this shit with me to make up for my shit past. I had nothing but respect for him, he was a straight up guy, do or die material is what I was dealing with here. "Fuck me Joe, don't be turning into a soft cunt on me." He placed his hand on my shoulder and turned his face towards me looking deep with his eyes, "no Kyle, I mean it, you're family to me, in fact we're thicker than blood could ever be. You've constantly proven yourself and I look forward to taking over this place with you. The balls on you kid, I can't believe you've got me taking on Henry Slate with you. Henry fucking Slate!"

Joe started the engine and drove towards Moss Side where we were to pick up the guns. I could tell there was a tear of emotion building up inside him, but he shrugged it off and smiled. "Well lad, I tell you what, they will write a book about you one day. Kyle Harrison taking on the biggest firm in Manchester, fuck me what a story." "Fuck a book, I'm thinking a feature film." We both laughed as we continued our journey.

I felt like I was in the forces again, that real sense of purpose that burns deep inside you and the desire to make shit happen. I was pumped up with adrenaline and was most definitely ready for action.

Past

The plan sounded simple in my head, but I knew there would be more at stake in reality. It had just been given the go ahead by the firm's leader Henry Slate and to be honest, whether he approved or not, I did not care. He was Henry and I was Kyle, two generations apart. I lay on my bed just imagining how things could turn out. I thought the best thing to do was to get them in the car and just execute them after a couple of drives around the block, but this wasn't an action movie, it was real life. I left the ending of the plan to Joe as I had done all the hard work, getting them together, so I felt at ease with that idea. Being unarmed didn't sit well with me though, 'come on,' I thought to myself, 'how can we kill them with no guns?' It did make me feel paranoid and it did not make sense how we were to complete our job. Joe did always find a way to surprise me but he had been in this game longer than I had, I was young and upcoming, but what I lacked in experience, I made up for in ideas and plans of how to pull a job off, which is why Joe most likely took a shine to me. I was grateful to be a part of the plan but not knowing how all of this was going to end made me paranoid. I did have faith in Joe, I just had to trust him and his ability to make this a successful plan.

The next day came and two Silver Shadow Rolls Royce motors arrived and parked outside the hotel. "Fuck me mate, this is a nice bit of kit." "Yeah it is mate." "How much does a beauty like this cost then?? Too much, you want a word of advice?" "What's Joe?" "Don't fall in love with these cars," he laughed to himself with bloodshot eyes. "Looks like you've been busy then with all this." A pause of silence came between us as Joe looked into the distance, his eyebrows lifted as he looked to me. "So, what's the plan then mate?" "The plan is for you is to stay cool

CHAPTER 11

and I'm thinking maybe you should sit this one out." "I'm not moving mate, we're sorting this shit out today. I want to see it done and done right." "I respect you kid, but you do know that things are going to turn ugly." "Well let's get to it, get that engine turned on and let's get heading off." "Right." Joe beeped his horn and waved his hand out of the window signalling towards one of his gang members behind him to start driving. "Who is he?" "An old friend you could say, that's all you need to know and stop asking me shit, we got to focus kid!"

Driving around in one of those cars was an experience in itself, the wheels hit the road so smoothly, you could tell it was a luxury car for sure. We headed in the direction of the train station. It wasn't too much of a long drive, so when we arrived we parked up and waited. I could feel each second ticking down and the suspense of the wait was brewing inside of me. Joe was quiet, he kept tapping his hands on the stirring wheel. For the first time, he had actually looked a bit on edge and this wasn't the Joe I knew. I could tell he was trying to play it cool and that he was secretly glad I was there. I was thinking passively to be honest with you, just people watching until the Jones twins and their protection came. We were expecting a pick-up of six people dressed in black and grey coloured clothes, smartly dressed and the typical cocky swag about them. After a good 20 minutes of silence, Joe broke it and flashed his lights at six figures. "There they are, the fucking scum." Joe muttered under his breath and opened his door. "Are you coming or what? Follow my lead." I jumped out of the car and walked behind Joe. "Alright boys! Welcome to Manchester." I could sense the fake enthusiasm of Joe's tongue speak the words into the air. It was so fake, even I could pick up on that. One of them leant forward and shook Joe's hand then swiftly pulled him in closer and started frisking him for weapons. Joe held his arms out with a grin on his face. "It's good to see you too, I've heard a lot about you." "And the lad, check him," one of the

Londoners from the Jones firm uttered, directing his attention towards me. I had never been searched before and to tell you the truth I just wanted to spit in this fucker's face. I obviously couldn't do anything, I just had to accept for this moment that I was a little mug. "Now that's a nice motor, isn't it boys?" Colin, one of the Jones twins, conveyed. "Yeah, it sure is," Rob Jones smiled. "So, lads, the Jones boys can ride with us and you can take the keys off my driver and drive the other motor and one things for certain, it's a smooth ride." "Sounds good!" The twins nodded like nodding dogs and jumped inside our car. "Lads, you best not crash, these beauties certainly don't come cheap!" "Yeah, you don't want to be doing that." Joe replied. "Mancos hey, they love their cars." I heard one snigger. "As do I," Colin responded.

"So, boys, what's your story, how come this lad is with you?" Rob scraped back his black gelled hair with his fingers. He had more weight on him than his brother Colin, the fat prick and I didn't like how this was going at all. Why would they ask these fucking questions? "So, lad, why are you here? What makes Henry choose you to pick us up?" "He's with me and Henry chose me to pick you up." "Oh, so you're his little bitch then?" For the first time of knowing Joe, I had never seen him take shit off anyone and in this moment, he completely changed and took it. It was a shock to the system for me to see, I don't care who they are, they come here on our side of the woods and disrespect us. It was bang out of order! "Yeah, that's right, I'm just a driver." "Well you fucking better get a move on, we don't have all day." "You're the boss!" I could tell it was hurting Joe as he gritted his teeth, but thankfully we weren't too far from our destination, just a couple of miles out of Manchester, near a warehouse was the meeting place. I assumed that Henry must have had a plan to have a shoot-out with them, it made sense going somewhere secluded.

CHAPTER 11

Thankfully, we eventually arrived at the location where Henry Slate was, team handed, after having to deal with annoying disrespectful small talk with the Jones twins. As we parked up, I was getting nervous inside, as I had no clue what was about to happen. I could feel myself shake slightly, hoping that Henry had a couple of snipers set up, pointing at the Jones twin's heads. I hoped for this so much, because I couldn't think of any other way we were going to get rid of them. Joe pressed the locks discretely on the doors and got out of his seat, I followed him as he got out. Joe popped his head into the car, "now lads, Henry is on his way, I'm just going to have a cigarette." "What do you mean, he's not fucking here?" Joe slammed the door in his face and shouted out to me, "RUN!" We started running and after a good 10 second sprint, I heard a huge explosion go off, then another. We ran towards a group of figures who happened to be Henry Slate and his crew. I was in shock, everything happened so fast, I didn't even have time to process what had just happened. I looked behind me and both cars were up in flames. I had no idea what had just happened, but to be fair, I'm glad it did. The silver-tongued London cunts deserved it. I could feel the heat from the fire and all I kept thinking was holy shit, that's one nasty way to go.

We eventually got within distance of Henry and his crew, I could hear them all cheering as Henry put his hand up and waved to me with a detonator in his hand. "Joe! You did it mate!" "Thanks, Henry pal." Joe and I were saturated in sweat and I could feel the adrenaline from the whole experience pound against my heart as I was still processing what the fuck had just gone on. "But guess what Joe, you've wasted a good 50 grand on them there motors and God knows what else, on the number of explosives you put in the boot for them fuckers." "It was the only way Henry." "Well, at least they can't come back from this and it sends a good message that we are not to be fucked with!" "It sure does Henry." "And who is this little bastard, why did you bring a boy into this?" "He's one of mine, in fact he gave me the idea." "Did he, you put your life in this kid's hands, to play gangster? That's very risky! Next time, just do it the old-fashioned way, will you?" "I'm hoping there won't be a next time Henry. These fuckers are dead and gone now." "Well, you're a reliable man so you don't know when I might need you."

I wiped the sweat from my face and kept my mouth shut. I was still in shock, I looked at Joe and he winked at me. "I told you I've got this." Indeed, he did and I guess I would have freaked out if I'd have known we were driving around with a bomb that could have gone up in smoke at any minute, but I guess that is the risk you take when you want more from life.

Present

We arrived outside a run down, knocked up house in Moss Side and as we sat there waiting for Joe's contact to open up his door, I fell into deep thought. I felt myself wonder was I really getting into Henry's head, I could not imagine the pain he must be going through but I know I had felt more over my life time. You can't change the facts of my past that still haunt me, but I was a man now, not a fucking kid and a man has got to do what he sets his heart out to do! For me, that was too fucking kill. My patience was wearing thin as I told Joe to give his contact another call. "Where the fuck is your guy? It will soon be morning and I want this done while we have the cover of night. Knock on will you!" "Right, fuck it, he should be here in a min, but yeah we'll knock on." "Good man, time is fucking precious." "Get the money out of the middle compartment mate." I pulled open the compartment of Joe's Range Rover and there were three envelopes filled thick with cash.

CHAPTER 11

This will do I thought, Joe had money everywhere and it was quite a good stash. I didn't even realize we were sat on grands. I got out of the car and tucked the money into my pockets, following behind Joe. He knocked on the door three times waiting for a response.

This big, black guy with a scar on his face opened the door, I had seen him before but I couldn't put a name to his face even though that scar is something you don't forget. He was Joe's contact, he had always used him for tools, "Terrell mate, where you been at, we've been waiting over fifteen minutes." "Sorry man, I was having a shit." I smirked in response to Terrell's honesty as he welcomed us inside. "It's the Macs you want, isn't it?" "Yeah, we need two Macs!" "Good because I've got just the ones you need; these little bastards spark more fire than bonfire night." "We'll take them! You heard anything on the streets then?" Joe spoke direct. "Well I've had an order from your Henry, I think something must be going down that's red hot, you know." 'Your Henry', I thought to myself! This Terrell had no clue what was happening on the streets, but he was right about one thing: it was hot and it was about to get hotter. It was best to keep this cunt in the dark, he had one sole purpose to provide us the merchandise and to keep his fucking mouth shut. "So where is my fucking money, I've got your gear here?" Terrell pulled open a black leather bag and inside was two Mac 11 Sub machine guns with two magazines. "I've thrown in two magazines for you both, but it's going to come at a cost you know that?" "Yeah, I know that. These fuckers best be ghosted untraceable!" "You know that I don't fuck about, only the best for my customers." "Right good," Joe looked at Terrell sternly and asked me for the money. "Here you go mate." "It best be all fucking there," Terrell snatched it from my hands and pointed his fingers at me. I thought it would have been easier to just add this cunt to the list of people we were going to wipe out as his disrespect was burning away inside of me. I had to stay cool though, he was not worth the loss of my focus. "Looks good," Terrell's eye's opened wide. "Right you guys best be off I've got to make some calls." "Okay mate." Joe and Terrell locked hands and I saw a smirk on Terrell's face. "I remember when this one was just a kid." "Well I'm not a fucking kid anymore, you best realise that." "The mouth on this one hey." "Take care Terrell, we're off and thanks for the tools." Joe picked up the leather bag and swung it over his shoulder. "Come on you!" Joe tried breaking my stare that I held at Terrell, the black fuck, who did he think he was? I was feeling trigger happy tonight and he was lucky I didn't turn on him. I was angry at the disrespect, but I had to calm my nerves. He wasn't on my 'to do' list yet, but I guess he was reliable in getting me what I wanted.

Past

A year of criminality passed and I was finally starting to become accepted as Joe's right hand man, but I kept thinking about the past and how far I had come on my journey. I had lost focus of why I was getting myself deeper into the rabbit hole of all of this. So, I decided if I was going to have the edge, I better get myself ready for the war I was about to start for myself. I had all this energy and frustration, so I had another one of my great ideas, I'd join the army. I wanted to know how it felt being in the ring with death brushing over your shoulder, the adrenaline rush pumping around your heart. It would help me get ready to tear up these streets, it would make me a real man who could command respect and have the edge on everyone. I felt bad leaving Spike behind, he had gone into boxing like he wanted and was working on the doors of some night clubs under the Chadds' protection. I didn't want him getting caught out or doing anything stupid, so I told Joe to keep an eye out for him as a favour. The last thing I wanted was seeing him get locked up when I got back from my first tour.

I needed the experience of becoming a professional killer and where better to become one, than in the armed forces. It's literally an all access pass to kill and get away with it, in fact you're awarded medals for that shit and called a hero. It was backwards when you think about it, but I didn't give a fuck. I was talking my street skills and killer instincts to the Falkland's. Fucking Argentinians didn't know what the fuck was coming.

FALKLANDS 1982

"Right boys, we're in enemy lines and this ain't no practice drill, shoot to kill!" My sergeant in command was Brett, he spoke with real grit. He was a real man, tough and not easily bruised, but one thing for certain, no matter who he thought he was, I was better. I had the fucking edge, because unlike all these other lads dressed in camo rags, I had seen things these fuckers only see in films and I had more than grit I had an FAL rifle that I was not scared of pulling the trigger on. Even though I had become close with my squad, there was one lad that stood out, his name was John, a younger private than me. He reminded me in a way of Spike, he took things so literal, it was kind of pathetic, but I didn't mind, I guess I have a soft spot for those who need someone to look out for them.

I was ready to take my first kill, I could see a group of the enemy soldiers gathering in the distance. We were in a concealed position in the mountains, but I couldn't help but want to pull the trigger, so I got the attention of Brett. "Let's fucking have them, they're in our sights." "Not yet Private." I hated being called Private, it was like being a kid again, being told what to do and even when to piss. I was my own man, there's only so many arses you can kiss in this journey to becoming a soldier and I had done my fair share in training. I got through with flying colours and was more than ready for the real deal, but now when the moment had arisen, being told 'no', pissed me off more than anything, so I did what Kyle does best and that was follow my own orders. I started firing off shots at the enemy, dropping some like flies whilst others were bunkering up. "WHAT THE FUCK ARE YOU DOING? GET BACK IN LINE, YOU HAVE GIVEN AWAY OUR POSITION!! CEASE FIRE!" "FUCK THIS, LADS LISTEN TO ME! THEY'RE FIRING BACK, GET THE FUCK DOWN AND PULL YOUR TRIGGERS!"

I felt the force of a hand pull me down to the ground. It was Brett and his face didn't look happy at all, but fuck Brett. He may have worn all the badges and stripes but I was the one really in charge here. "Get the fuck off me! Can't you see we are in the middle of a fire fight?" "You disrespected a direct order! You little fucker!" Brett pulled his pistol on me and screamed in my face, but it was muffled in the sound of gun shots. "When we get out of this, you'll see what happens to you!" This cunt had nearly got me killed, I could feel the bullets firing back at me, ricocheting over my head. I pushed Brett off me and gripped firmly onto my rifle aiming it at the enemy for the second time. BANG! BANG! BANG! I fired off my rifle as quickly as possible and reloaded it as quick as my hands would let me. I kept emptying my magazine at the enemy until it went silent. I was lucky that we didn't lose anybody, I could feel my blood pumping and the face of Brett was abhorrent. This wasn't my first encounter with the enemy, but this time I'm sure glad we made a mess, as last time things got intense and that shit stays with you. When you kill a man with your bare hands, that's the kind of shit that fucks with your head at night. As I was pulling the trigger I kept

CHAPTER 11

thinking to myself I won't end up in that position again.

Brett approached me at the camp we had set up, "Listen to me son, you're not cut out for this, you nearly got us all killed out there. You freaked out and we can't have freak outs like that again. You will end up costing us lives and your behaviour is out of control since your last incident just last week." "You don't understand man, they're out there Brett, they're fucking out there and I will kill them all." "You're not mentally stable Kyle. I give the orders for a reason, I can't risk you fucking up. Pack your bags tonight because you're flying out tomorrow and I'm going to have to take that gun off you. I don't trust you freaking out at the sound of a bang again." "Fuck off Brett, I can't sleep without it." "Well you're going to have to mate, you'll be out of here tomorrow."

Present

Once again, I followed behind Joe and jumped back inside the car, I took the bag of guns off Joe and put them by my feet. I leant over and looked once again inside the bag at the guns. I felt the grip of them and I could feel that sensation of power you get when you are behind a trigger. Tonight was going to be fun, I could not wait, it had been a long time since I had used a gun like this and the adrenaline you get from it is a sensation that stays with you. I was excited to pull the trigger, but I wanted to send a message. Something to really impact Henry that he had never experienced before. A drive by was still just a drive by, so I told Joe what I was thinking. "You know what mate, I need to get my hands on a brick." "Of coke?" His face looked confused. "No, I mean a real brick or a big fucking stone, something I can throw through the bar's window." "Oh, right, why?" "Because I'm going to wrap a message around it." "Oh right, I thought the hit was a message in itself." "Well this makes it more personal," I spoke calmly but I could feel the tension building up in my body. I could feel this was all going to come to an end soon, I could taste it in the air, it was real and this was just going to be the icing on the cake, letting loose on this fucker's place. I felt like a soldier again, except this time I was fighting in my own army, even if it was an army of two right now but I did have some lads lined up on the blower.

This was just for me and Joe to do, we were on the frontline of the streets and we owned them. "Right, get me a brick then." It was around 4am in the morning and the roads were quiet for now, I told Joe to park outside a random house not far from the pub so I could grab a brick or stone from someone's garden. I found a half-broken brick, this would do the job. "Fuck me, its freezing, turn the bastard heater on mate, its fucking cold out there!" Joe laughed to himself and shared his thoughts, "I've never seen you this excited over a brick before, you're like a fucking kid!" "Haven't you ever bricked a window in your time?" "When I was a kid yeah, I was fucking thirteen, not a fucking man," Joe laughed and to be fair I could see the humour in it. What was I thinking, throwing a fucking brick, but once I had something in my head I had to follow it through. I got some tissue from my pocket and grabbed a pen that was in the middle compartment. I thought for a moment and then wrote, 'if you're reading this, I guess you're still alive but don't worry you won't be soon! I'm coming for you! Looks like the chess pieces are in my favour, you have nowhere to hide!' I read my words out loud and thought 'yeah, it sounds about right'. "Fuck me, you are creative," Joe spoke as I wrapped the tissue around the brick. "Shut the fuck up bro, this is Psychological Warfare 101".

Finally, we were ready to take action. I looked at Joe and gave him the nod, whilst inside I felt a sense of excitement as the journey I had been on had been long and I knew if one of these bullets hit Henry that would be it, game fucking over. I wasn't being too optimistic as I knew this cunt was a tough bastard and had more lives that a cat. I remained steady and calmed my nerves with a cigarette. "Let's have it Joe, let's make this fucking special." I pulled the Macs from the leather bag and loaded the magazines, 32 shots ready to burst, I smiled to myself taking a drag on the cigarette. A lot of blood had already been spilled so far, but you know what, it had been worth it, every action to move forward. Leading up to these moments I wanted to put so much fear into Henry and make him pay for every second of pain he had caused me. "Let's get this done." I pulled back the slide on the guns and locked them off, all ready to explode, passing one of the Macs over to Joe. Joe put his foot on the gas and I threw the cigarette out of the window. I had one hand on the brick and the other on the Mac. I see Joe's eyes light up just like mine, but he went quiet, he had more of a relationship than I had with Henry over the years, but he was loyal to me now but I could understand that it must have been a bit of a head fuck for him, but we were brothers in arms and his word was his word.

We were getting closer to the pub and I could feel my hands twitch on the grips. To feel a sense of nerves was new to me, but you know what, I reckon it must have been the reality of the situation I was now in, all finally sinking in, but at this moment in time I had to keep focused and ignore my emotions. In this game emotions were a sure thing to get you killed and tonight I wasn't going to let that happen. We had the element of surprise at our advantage. I turned on Joe's CD player and a track hit as we moved closer and closer. 50 Cent's 'Many Men' started to play as I jumped into the back seat and wound the window down facing the street side where the pub was. Joe looked at me from the wing mirror and gave me the nod. I gripped hard on the

Mac and sprayed simultaneously with Joe's rounds. BANG! BANG! BANG! BANG! The bullets screeched all along the pub's front entrance, smashing and shattering all of the windows. Joe's car came to a stop as I jumped outside, still spraying away, with one hand on the Mac and the other holding the brick. I threw the brick straight through the window and fired until my Mac locked empty. I turned back and started running towards Joe's car as the sound of six shots went off in my direction. One flew past my leg and hit the car door. Fuck me, I was lucky, I nearly got clipped. I jumped in the back seat and kept my head down as I shouted drive to Joe. "Get a fucking move on! That cunt nearly took my leg clean off." Joe turned the music down and started laughing hysterically. "Who the fuck does he think he is, Clint fucking Eastwood? I'll tell you what, that was lucky!" "Aw you're funny, you man, you should have seen your face as you were running back, it was like something off Mission Impossible." "Shut the fuck up bro!" I climbed back into the front of the car and threw the smoking gun into the bag. "Do you think he got the message?" "Yeah, I think he got the message alright!" Joe stepped on the gas and winked at me, "I think you've just awoken the giant mate, we might be fucked now, he has a full team hand and we're just a couple of lads if the others have been dealt with." "Well, least he has nowhere to hide now. He loved that bar and now it's fucked!"

"Yeah, but so are we." "Don't lose confidence in us bro, we're soldiers. I know what I'm doing," I smiled and zipped the bag up. "Soldiers of the streets and I'm the fucking general." "Well, when all of this is done and dusted I'm wearing the fucking crown, you know that." "We'll rule this city together mate and expand the firm." "Will still have to deal with all the others who are with Henry though." "Yeah but when he's gone, things will fall into place. Being at war is bad for business, we will come to an agreement, I'm sure of it." "If not, we will have cut the head off the snake." "Yeah that's true." Joe agreed. "A disorganised group is no match for fearlessness, I'll kill every one of them!"

CHAPTER 11

I sat there feeling the physical motion of movement from the car. Being at one with every vibration and bump, I went into deep thought. I started to reminisce on the past and how far I had come. Even though my grandmother was a good woman with strong ethics, I still think a part of her would have been proud. Okay, maybe not the fact that I am the man I am today, although I have become this person through her and the circumstances I experienced, but the fact that I was doing something for her, in her memory, was something one day when I meet her in the heavens, she will be proud of. Then again, I don't think I will be going to heaven. I smiled to myself, at least it will be warmer where I am going.

This cat and mouse chase was starting to grind on me, so I sent Henry a text, 'let's just fucking meet, man to man, old school. Here's a picture of your favourite girl!' I attached a picture of his dead daughter on my bed, it did put a grin on my face. Fucking with his head was an endless joy of mine but it was time to end this cunt. I couldn't think of a fairer option than to meet. There were questions I wanted to ask this cunt that had been brewing in my mind ever since I was a kid.

Past

I arrived on home soil with a medical discharge, they said I was mentally unstable and had a diagnosis of PTSD. What the fuck did they know, at least I was back and experienced in killing, something the lads back home couldn't knock me for. I doubt any of them had killed as many fuckers as me. In the line of duty hey, my arse, fuck them and fuck them all. Mental health conditions, I was as normal as they come, they were just soft. All of them soft cunts don't know what it takes to have that killer instinct. Now I was back and ready to take on my own mission, to find this bastard who fucked up my life from the start. I had grown so much as a person and I was looking forward to seeing Joe and Spike, to share with them my stories and catch up on what was going on and then to start the hunt for the man who brought me on this journey. I was ready to take over for certain, I was home.

Present

Now growing up I was a good kid and didn't do anything wrong, but as a man I had broken every moral that I had been given, that would take me down a journey to these moments in my life. I was beginning to become impatient, it was time to prepare for a meet with Henry. I wasn't stupid but I definitely was letting my guard down slightly as I text him an address of an abandoned mill in Chadderton. "We might need some lads Joe, I need you to get two of your best gunmen to meet us at the mill in Chadderton and we need to move fast!" "Hang on a minute, what?" "I've just text Henry and told him we will meet today." "Don't you want to wait a few days and gather your thoughts?" "No Joe, we have got to strike while the iron is hot!" "We have not even slept; don't you want to sleep on it?" "No Joe! We have got to take action now, while he is weak we will meet him. We're younger than he is, he won't be able to think clearly. I can't give him time to think and rebuild himself." "Right, well okay! I'll make the calls."

I knew Joe was half asleep and tired from being on the go the past few days but I couldn't wait. Maybe it was my psyche from being in the army, spending days on end watching the enemy and just like my enemies in war, this was my war on the streets and Henry was more than an enemy, he was my fuel to kill. My entire motivation and purpose came down

CHAPTER 11

to these moments in my life. I was not just satisfied with killing the Connolly brothers, I wanted to destroy the full root of the tree and the true responsible one for my grandmother's death. Blood would always be thicker than water, but I had no blood left, except from the bond I had with Spike and Joe. They were my brothers and to be fair I had not heard from Spike but I couldn't let my concerns distract me from my main focus. Today was going to be the day, I could feel it in my gut. Only one outcome and one aim: to kill Henry Slate!

An hour or two passed and we had rounded up two other lads for the job and we got to the mill first. I told the lads to get their hands on some spray paint and get some pictures printed of Henry's daughter. I wanted to leave a treat for him, I stuck the pictures on the walls inside the mill. I wanted to constantly remind him what it was like to lose a loved one and to feel that pain before we met face to face. I had no remorse. Why should a man of his status live like a king for all these years, whilst I live in the shadows waiting for my moment to shine? Well I'll tell you what, there was nothing he could do or say to get in my head, he had already made a hole in my heart and as the moments passed I could feel it heal. I was very close to fulfilling my promise that I made to myself all those years ago.

I tried to phone Spike but still there was no answer, I thought I could have used him at a time like this, as he had been through the same journey as me. Then I thought, I'm like his big brother, would you really bring your little bro with you, to a showdown like this was going to be. I took a moment to think and then thought something might be up. "Hey lads, have you heard anything from Spike?" I questioned the two lads who had come down to lend a hand. "Nah, not seen him our kid." One of them responded whilst the other shook his head. The thoughts of 'where the fuck is he?' ran through my mind as Joe interrupted me. "Don't worry about him, you need to focus bro. They could arrive any minute. You need a clear head." He was right, I did need to relax myself, as my nerves were already high.

I held my Glock with a gently grip and pointed it towards the two lads who had joined us. "You best lock and load boys or otherwise I'll make you go night, night, myself. Get yourselves ready and for fuck sake bally the fuck up!" I could feel the energy inside me brewing as I was beginning to lose patience. "They will be here, trust me Kyle." "Well the clock is ticking and I can feel every second." The atmosphere was quiet until I heard the sound of creaking footsteps. Joe whispered, "they're coming up the stairs." I felt the sweat drizzle down the side of my face as my senses opened up to every sound.

I aimed my Glock towards the entrance and slipped my finger around the trigger. Ready, for at any moment, to let it explode. Reality was starting to kick in and my arm slightly shook. "Fuck me!" I mumbled to myself. Was this really happening, I could not believe I was moments away from a face-off with Henry Slate. Three silhouettes appeared in the dark and was lit by the twinkling of a light that shown Henry's face. "I'm glad you could make it," I spoke assertively with an angered undertone. He responded and acknowledged me. He too held his antique revolver at me with a glare of vengeance in his eye. I could taste the emotions of anger that loomed in the air from reading his face, as he read mine. Amongst the conversation and the silence, over a thousand words were spoken, but between us, we both heard exactly what was needed. His face was wrinkled and I could see the tiredness in him, he was a worn out old man. He coughed and spat blood onto the floor, I had no empathy for the old cunt, not one bit. He had destroyed my life and I was glad to return the favour.

CHAPTER 11

I had some pictures in my pocket of my family, I wanted him to see the pain he had caused and a reminder to him that he was no saint. We were the same, or in fact I was better than him, but I kept them in my pocket until the moment was right. "My grandmother was pure and you took her away from me, you mother fucker. You don't realise the pain you caused an innocent young child. I was a fucking kid and you took everything away from me. For what? Money? Some fucking quick cash? Well guess what, I'm glad your daughter is dead and she loved every second of her time with me. Before I pulled the trigger on her she begged like a bitch for her life and you know what, all whilst my cock was inside her." I expressed my anger viciously and I could tell he wanted to blow my fucking head off right there and then. I revealed the photos, "you see this, at least I recognise who I kill. You probably don't even recognise these people and you won't, because they were my family. My mother, my gran and me, you took all I had left." Henry cocked the hammer on his revolver and moved closer to me, it made me feel agitated but I didn't care, I was ready, more than fucking ready. He knelt down and picked up the photographs. I could sense confusion in his face as his eyes scanned left to right. "Fuck me! Fuck me! What's your mother called?" He spoke gently with a firm touch. I see his eyes widen with an overwhelming expression on his face. "Vicky! Why you ask?" Sweat dripped down my hand and I could feel it on the palms of my grip. "What do you know of your father?" "I know nothing of my father other than he was never in my life," I responded feeling confused by all the random questions. Joe pulled off his balaclava and shouted directing his voice towards Henry. "What the fuck has all of this got to do with anything?" "No fucking way Joe, what the fuck! I looked to you as a son, how could you be involved in this?" "I don't think that matters old man, what matters is here and now." "YOU FUCKING TRAITOR!" Henry screamed in Joe's face following the insults from Jason and Sam. Everyone's fingers were on their triggers from both sides as I was trying to understand what Henry's connection was to the photos, my mother and me. "Your name's Kyle, isn't it?" Henry wiped the sweat from his head with his free hand and with his other he pointed his gun down slightly then back up towards my head. "You're one of mine! You're my son! I thought your mother had an abortion!" I could not believe what had just come out of his mouth. I was angry but confused at the same time, I told myself in those moments it was not true. "You fucking liar, you're not my fucking dad, you're a crazy old man! YOU ARE NOT MY BLOOD!!" I raised my Glock and pointed it right between Henry's eyes. "ARGH!!" I shouted at the top of my lungs, expressing all the pain I was experiencing. "YOU ARE NOT MY FUCKING DAD!" tears started to stream down my face. I can't be, I can't be, I kept telling myself, I could not have raped and murdered my own sister. Everything was so fucked up beyond repair and the only way out was through pulling this trigger. BANG!

Chris Slate

I could feel it in the water and knowing my brother this was not going to end well. All these years by his side and only time would tell when my protection would run out and Henry would meet his match. I walked into this abandoned warehouse where passers-by had heard gun shots. With the fire arms squad beside me and a Glock pistol in my hand, leading this team was almost as intimate as the brotherhood my brother had created. But we were the men in blue, we were on the right side of the fence. I could feel the sweat ripple down my face as I knew this sit down had not gone well for Henry. It was a sick sense I was experiencing, the feeling of knowing before seeing the reality of the situation. My grip started to slip slightly on my Glock with the sweat on

CHAPTER 11

the palm of my hand, my nerves were getting the better of me. "Seven fatalities down," John spoke assertively aiming his G36C at the bodies. I put my arm on top of his gun pointing it down towards the floor. John looked at me knowing who was lay on the floor. "Area secure," he radioed to the team. I continued to walk amongst the bodies.

There lay my brother, my big brother. Sickness struck me as I witnessed the blood and grey, lifeless face. I knelt down on one knee and stared into his open eyes. Tears began to fall discreetly on my right cheek. "If only you would let me in brother," I whispered under my breath. They say we all have our day, but he knew it would end like this. I closed Henry's eyes with my hand as I heard John mutter on the radio. "We haven't got long before the full team are here." I stood up to see what all the fuss was about and there too lay Kyle Harrison, he had been on our radar for a while. I watched a pool of blood flow, my eyes followed it too his face. Breathing ever so slowly on his last breath, Kyle whispered with a smile, "and now you feel my pain Detective Slate." His smile slowly relaxed with a spark in his eye as he died. Determined, I thought, holding back my pain and anger. I loved my brother and this evil bastard lay here, but in the bible, it did say, you reap what you sow and this was all in the harvest for my brother Henry Slate. Son of a bandit just as me.

The End

Authors Interview

What is your truth on writing?

Anything that is challenging in life requires solitude and a teaspoon of loneliness with constant discipline, to acquire the success that we aspire for. When I started writing it was purely for something to prove, that I could create something and do the impossible and break the rules. I had never actively sought to read books and there I was writing my first one, with no idea what I was doing but holding pure faith into my imagination and that one day knowing I would get to my last sentence.

15 years of age my journey began and I was ambitious but frustrated with my circumstances. My escape was writing on the bus to and from college on a throw away phone. If it was not for my own discipline back then that I had acquired from a young age I would not have been able to conquer this voyage of applying my imagination to paper and these words I write now would not exist.

The truth with myself is, I do not know how to write as no one ever sat down with me to teach me how to do it. What I have learnt is that the most important thing for new writers like myself, or anyone who wants to acquire some kind of achievement, is the importance of the mind-set and rituals we endure ourselves to go through. Life with goals is exciting but extremely challenging, you just have to grit your teeth and push through with your mind. It's your mind that is the most powerful tool that allows us to create and you must protect it from people who don't see the value in what you do. Just like 'Jenga' the higher you build your metaphorical tower the easier it is to fall down. You have got to use all the tools you can, to cement the fact you are not going backwards.

Also, to new writers, dreamers, goal seekers and ambitious, creative people, being alone with yourself to create worlds that don't exist in reality is a demanding lifestyle choice, as we carry the characters we create. Our imaginations never switch off so when you're out with friends and you get that feeling of a great idea emerge for a scene in your story or a feature to your product, remember it's only you that you can share the truth with. Not everyone you meet will share the same excitement for your thoughts when they come, as in their eyes it may not be cool. So, keep your ideas close and trust your instincts because creative work is a very subjective field to be within. You should be proud that you're in motion with pursuing something that will leave an impact. However big or small, it still will impact those around you and your future children as you leave something physical behind. That's one of the core values of my truth as a writer, author, creative, storyteller or whatever the title I acquire, may be. It's the impact you have and leave.

How do you create your stories?

To be honest with you, I always find this question a hard one as I don't always have the best answer, but I just trust in my imagination and over time a story can grow in your mind. I wrote the first few scenes of this book 2 years before I started to focus on the full manuscript. I started it as an experiment to try a new form and style of writing and showed it to my dad, he took to the first scene and from there on, my imagination started to open up to what I could create.

Why do you write crime novels?

Well this is an interesting question indeed, I guess it comes from favouring crime films when I was younger and hearing some stories growing up on the adventures of my grandad. These inspired the stories I created, even though they are fiction and simply all created with imagination. One day I wish to write a real story based on my grandfather's life as I have always been fascinated with hearing the folk tales passed down through my family about his adventures.

Printed in Poland
by Amazon Fulfillment
Poland Sp. z o.o., Wrocław